THE LAST DANCE OF GUS FINLEY

A Tale of Eastern Kentucky Justice

By John Sparks

Old Seventy Creek Press
P. O. Box 204
Albany, Kentucky 42602

ISBN: 1442108827   EAN-13: 9781442108820

Front Cover Photo the Rockhouse arch by Peter Owen

To die, to sleep—

To sleep, perchance to dream—ay, there's the rub;

For in that sleep of death what dreams may come

When we have shuffled off this mortal coil

Must give us pause.

—*Shakespeare,* Hamlet

ACKNOWLEDGMENTS

This book is a work of historical fiction. As such, though it is based on actual events that occurred in eastern Kentucky more than a century ago, I must state as a matter of record that its plot and characterizations should not be taken in any sense as serious history—at least, no more so than, say, the novels of Thomas Wolfe. But as a writer much better than myself once observed, there is always the chance that such a book of fiction may throw some light on what has been written as fact. I hope that it is so.

Thanks to the staff of the Johnson County Public Library of Paintsville, Kentucky, for reference access to their

Patton Room and its extensive collection of historical documents, including compiled and reprinted records of Floyd and Johnson County, Kentucky court proceedings of yesteryear—and regional historian Henry P. Scalf's invaluable *Kentucky's Last Frontier,* wherein is chronicled the true story of the events here portrayed.

Thanks to Laura Sutton of the University Press of Kentucky for reading the manuscript and offering several helpful comments and suggestions. Many more thanks to Rudy Thomas of Old Seventy Creek Press for invaluable editorial input, and guidance in polishing the work.

Thanks to Rev. Johnnie Ross, now of Lexington, Kentucky, for the anecdote about the rope in the old Floyd County courthouse. *Sic transit gloria mundi.*

And thanks most especially to the farmers, hunters, livestock traders, teachers, preachers, soldiers, and story tellers who settled Greasy Creek and made it their own, the dust from whence I came, and to their descendants still living there, the dust to which I shall return.

The Author

CHAPTER ONE

The light of gray dawn shone dully though the open barn door, and Frank squinted a bit as he groped at the peg on the wall for the right size bridle for his horse. Hen had always fussed at him for hanging up his plow rigging and saddle tack in an inconsistent manner, and this morning he wished for once that he'd gone along with the older man's nagging to keep everything in its proper place. The horse was twenty, a year older than Frank and a little swaybacked, but he could still pull a plow and accommodate a saddle well enough, so his owner knew he had no right to complain. Besides, it was Frank's own, bought with money he had earned himself by trading, and whatever he might do with the horse was his own business. Still, he glanced enviously over to the two other stalls at Hen's sleek, fine bay mares. His adopted father made his living at cattle and horse trading and he was good at it; he could afford to feed his saddle horses ten ears of corn three times a day, thrice an ordinary stock animal's diet, and they showed it. Frank let out a mirthless snort. The brutes had better be well fed if they were going to carry Hen to the Mount Sterling and Flemingsburg stockyards where he made most of his money. Hen had not been nicknamed Fat for no reason. Squat, stumpy little Henderson Harman measured five feet three inches and once weighed in on a livestock scale at two hundred eighty pounds. Although he could set a horse with the best, he was too corpulent to dismount with a shred of grace. He simply rolled off his saddle and lay on the ground until Maw Jane, Mary, or Frank himself took the exhausted animal to the barn and came back to help him up. But had not the pride of being a grown man now with a wife and baby son of his own prevented Frank from doing so, he would have begged the loan of one of the mares for today's occasion.

His hand closed around a leather strap of the bridle he wanted, an old-style cavalry model, and in an instant he began to try to fit it over his aged gelding's head. The nag was cranky this morning, having pulled a plow for Frank and his friend Richard Sparks from sunup till dusk the day before. It tossed its head back and forth with an irritated nicker and a snap of its long teeth. Immediately, Frank gave the lines to his temper. His face contorted with a rage he could not control. He raised the bridle, determined to strike the animal across its swayed back, but he stopped the motion in midair. He couldn't afford to let the iron bit, or even a ring or buckle on the bridle, make a gash on the horse. He had made a similar mistake once with a jack when he was younger, and had walked rather than ridden until Hen's homemade oak-ooze lotion had had a chance to heal the stubborn little nag's "fistulow," as his foster father had called the wound. Hen had groused about the donkey's back long after the animal had proven its restored good health by the fathering of mules, but Frank himself could remember the time Hen himself had flown angry and bitten his own prize mount on the nose when it nipped his arm. In that incident, the horse had unwittingly gotten its revenge by jerking back and upward, knocking out one of Hen's front teeth. The moon-faced little stockman could be hard to cipher sometimes.

Frank dropped the bridle and looked wildly about for some place to vent. It was lucky that none of the pups that Hen's white feist bitch had recently dropped were weaned and able to roam much yet. If one had been heedless enough to get close to him at that moment he'd have killed it without batting an eye.

Finally he clenched his right fist and delivered a haymaker to the poplar wall of the barn. Unconcerned, the old horse merely dropped its head again while Frank's anger spent itself quickly as he stooped over, swearing at the wood, the horse, and himself under his breath as he sucked at his bruised knuckles.

Although Frank's temper never seemed to erupt so violently when he had to deal with grown men his own size or bigger, or anything else that had the power to return his blows, he hardly ever reflected on it. In truth he never reflected on anything much, period, unless he had to. He just knew that his anger was quick and intense, and accepted it and pretty much expected everyone around him to accept it as well. It was just the way he was, for some reason, and if that meant nursing a swollen knuckle or two or knocking out a recalcitrant stock dog's brains on a fence post from time to time that's just how things were. He'd heard his half-sister whisper to Hen and Jane that his temper was his only inheritance from his real father, the preacher down below the Three Forks of Greasy. At a church service some twenty years previously the widowed minister had smiled and shaken the hand of a deliciously pretty young Pike

County woman who had come to visit her brother and sister-in-law in Johnson County, and afterward had ordered that his name be taken off the congregation's record book so that he might seduce her without the congregation's censure. No one was sure whether her Confederate soldier husband had died on some battlefield or simply skipped the country after the War Between the States, and under such circumstances the preacher couldn't possibly marry her and return to any sort of good standing with the church.

Not that she had needed all that much encouragement to become a kept woman at least for a little while. The War had left its own special legacy of despair and bitterness on her and countless girls just like her all over eastern Kentucky, and conventional morality was then only beginning to come back into fashion.

Her dead or deserted husband had already given her one small daughter to feed; she'd had to make a living somehow, and with the wayward minister she was at least better off than all the mountain girls and women in similar situations who had had to hire themselves out as so-called laundresses for militia companies during the War and for timber crews after it was over.

Uncle Billy Sparks, Richard's father and Hen's good friend who lived over on Pigeon Roost Fork, had brought home a dose of the pock that he'd acquired from just such an unfortunate while on duty in the Confederate Army. He still suffered from occasional outbreaks of it twenty years later, even after he'd seen the light and joined the church and one of his sons had become a preacher. Nobody knew whether the disease had had anything to do with either the untimely death of his wife Elizabeth a month ago, or the fits of madness that periodically seized his son Dan. Frank and Hen had once had to help Uncle Billy and his other sons drag logs over the mouth of a well that Dan had tried to jump in, and for all their labor the frantic Dan had simply flung the heavy beech logs off the well mouth single-handedly, as if they were matchsticks, before the harried Sparks family got him back under control. But good neighbors didn't ask questions of such a personal nature even among their own families in the privacy of their homes. The War had affected everybody, some more, some less.

The girl had borne Frank for the preacher and then another daughter for some man down on Big Sandy, but now she was respectably married again back in Pike or Martin County one or the other. The preacher was remarried too, forgiven and once again exhorting his congregants on Two Mile and Greasy Creeks to be followers of him even as he was of Christ, and Frank had been with Henderson and Jane Harman here at the mouth of Yost

Branch since he was four years old. His younger half-sister Nancy had stayed off and on with Hen and Jane too, but she was sixteen now and, in an ironic twist of fate, she had gotten the preacher (who happened to be her sweetheart's brother-in-law by the minister's much-younger second wife) to assume her guardianship so that her swain could court her without Hen's complaints. The preacher had a great reputation as a man of God. Only Nancy, his own wife and family, and those living within about a mile of his home really knew of the temper that the minister had unknowingly and uncaringly passed on to his bastard and some of his legitimate children as well, mostly from being able to hear the slap of leather and hickory and screams in the distance. Spare the rod and spoil the child was the rule of the Old Testament, and it was said that this religious man did dearly love to obey the commandments of God.

The cows on the other side of the big barn lowed plaintively. Frank hated to leave them uncomfortable, but he didn't have time this morning to milk them and set them out to pasture. Hen'd be grumbling about that too, of course, but Maw Jane was a better hand at milking than either he or Hen was anyway. The horse now for some reason decided to be tractable, and as Frank secured the bridle and saddle he thought of the day, fifteen years ago, that he had come to live with the good-hearted couple who had given him their surname as his own.

In his earliest childhood he'd been knocked from pillar to post and back again. He'd lived for a time with his mother, whose youthful beauty he dimly recalled, then one family and another who had grudgingly kept him. He'd been alternately starved and fed scraps left behind by legitimate children until he suffered from malnutrition so badly that he'd become jaundiced and his belly had swollen so big he could hardly toddle around on his little legs. Somehow he'd wound up with Jim Hawkum Ward and his wife Martha over on Hurricane, but since they already had one daughter of their own they'd agreed to let the childless Henderson and Jane Harman take him.

Jim Hawkum had walked him into the woods one day, turned his head and said to him, "Run on up ahead there, Frank, Daddy has to piss."

When he'd climbed and scampered through a clump of brush to a clearing, there had been Maw Jane, smiling and waiting on him with a small sack of clothing and baked goods, and a little dog. He eagerly accepted the little bundle, the first present he had ever received, and when Maw Jane had asked him if he would like to be her little boy he'd had no qualms about replying, "I will, if I can carry this little budget and you carry me."

So Maw Jane had borne him homeward to Yost Branch, the pup trotting behind them and wagging his tail, and she and Hen had been kindness itself to him. They gave him a name, a home, good nutritious meals, and a lot of love. Hen was jolly and full of jokes and his occasional blustering rages were even comical, like the time he bit the horse and lost a tooth. Folks couldn't help but laugh at him, and then he'd get tickled at his own actions and laugh along with them. Besides scolding, the only thing resembling real punishment he'd ever given the boy was once for ruining a pelt he was attempting to tan. He'd slapped Frank across the shoulder a few times with the flimsy, barely cured hide, and he and his adopted son both had a laugh about it afterward. As Frank grew into his teens and Hen occasionally found himself irked at an adolescent's misadventures, he'd simply slap his own massive thigh and growl, *"By the livin', Frank, what have you done now?"*

Frank smiled at the memories as he mounted the old horse and eased it down the slope from the barn to the house. The grin wasn't too wide, though. From years of practice he stifled it, biting his upper lip in the hope that the downy mustache that he was trying to establish there had grown a bit overnight. Frank had a slight birth defect, an extremely thick upper lip that folded back grotesquely in its middle when he smiled, doubling into what looked almost like two separate upper lips. From a distance he almost looked hare lipped when he grinned broadly. Though it didn't impede his speech he was extremely self-conscious about it, and he hoped that once he could grow his mustache out to the current fashion and completely cover his mouth he might not be subject to any more ridicule about the anomaly. The tough Confederate veterans on upper Greasy, few of whom had ever seen a slave, let alone owned one, could tease cruelly, and none of them were either small or weak enough for a showing of his anger.

It was important to his dignity as a grown man to keep that ugly upper lip covered, he knew. No one had been more surprised than he was when pretty, dark Mary Ann Elizabeth Viers, Jim Hawkum and Martha's niece back over on Hurricane, had found him attractive, except when her parents, Wash and Cynthia, had consented to their marriage even though they were completely aware that he'd been a woods colt and a less than handsome one to boot. Wash's grandmother had been baseborn too, and Wash himself had a couple of sisters who had been victimized by the War as much as Frank's real mother had. Wash and Cynthia made him every bit as much at home as Hen and Jane, and Cynthia

25

assured him that his real mother's people, acquaintances of her own dead Confederate soldier first husband before the War, were as fine and upstanding a family as could be found in the hills until four long hard years of brother fighting against brother had reduced nearly everyone to depravity and desperation. According to Cynthia, though, if not Wash too, it was all the Yankees' fault. She was as staunch a Confederate as most of her brothers were Unionists.

Wash even secured the services of old Preacher Jim Williamson from over in Martin County to perform the wedding since it was obvious that they couldn't ask Frank's real father, and Frank and Mary had begun their married life in Wash and Cynthia Viers' crowded little cabin at the head of Hurricane. Their son George— George Washington, named for Wash— had been born there seven months ago, and only at the start of planting season this year had Frank returned, with his bride and baby, to Hen and Jane's hospitality once more. Hen was trying to teach Frank the business of cattle and horse trading, so he could establish himself on his own.

Henderson Harman opened his cabin door and waddled onto his front porch, a pair of big milk buckets in his hands, when Frank rode up to the side of the porch on the old gelding.

"I see you left this for me and your ma to do," he said by way of greeting. "Bet you didn't feed my horses nor nothin' else neither. You had time to bath and dress up and slick your hair, though, and be out and gone 'fore your ma had breakfast served up."

"Seen John yet?" Frank returned, parrying the accusations.

Hen snorted. "Naw, I ain't," he replied crossly, "and if he's got any sense I won't this early. For the life of me I cain't figure why you boys got to gallivant all the way to Prestonsburg to watch that thing."

Frank colored a bit. "It's a big event," he retorted. "Somethin' that don't happen ever' day, and I want to see it. You brought the first news about it home yourself when you was up that way tradin'! Me and Dick Sparks plowed all durn day yesterday just tryin' to catch my work up so I could go."

"Yeah, and you and him run my last plow point plumb dull a-doin' it too, just like all the others," Hen countered. "You could stay around today and sharpen 'em, you know. Besides, one of them cows has got the greasy heel, and I could use your help doctorin' it. Maybe I can get Dick to come up and help me with the cow and the plow points. I know for a fact he ain't goin'."

"Well, no, I reckon not," Frank replied. "I asked him about it yesterday and he just looked funny and didn't say nothin'. Figgered some way it might of made him feel sad about Aunt Betty's funeral again—"

Hen put down the buckets and slapped his thigh with his characteristic motion of irritation.

"By the livin'," he thundered, "hain't you got a lick of sense at all? It was Dick's cousin down at Ashland two years ago that—"

Frank lowered his head. "Oh, good Lord, I clean forgot," he muttered. "I'll bet you he's told Uncle Billy and ever' one of the other boys we're goin', and me and John's gotta ride right up through there to meet Lee."

Henderson's jowls wobbled in disgust. "Look," he said. "Me and Bill Sparks likes to have a joke on each other as good as ary men, but I'd ruther cut my own tongue out as to hurt him or a one of them boys. Betty hain't been dead a month yet and here you've probably got 'em all tore up again. If you don't stay home and mind your own business, I'll always think you ort to. I'm surprised Wash Viers'd let Lee go."

Frank started to answer, but at that moment Hen's nephew John Addington came into sight from the bend in the creek, urging his mule along. When he got closer, they saw he was grinning, with his hair slicked back and dressed in his best, just like Frank was. As Frank and his foster father dropped their dispute to hail the new arrival, Maw Jane came out to join her husband and son, holding baby George and patting his back. Eighteen year-old Mary followed, demurely buttoning the top button of her dress; the baby had just finished drinking his breakfast, and Maw Jane was burping him for her.

Mary gave her young husband a slight smile. "You bound to go?" she asked in her laconic, low-timbre voice.

Frank nodded stiffly, a bit embarrassed. A year younger than he, Mary had always seemed more mature. She could always get the best of him in a husband-wife spat without even raising her voice, and for all the harshness of his temper he didn't dare hit her. Besides the fact that such an act of violence would cause Maw Jane to cry and Hen to storm, Mary was the oldest daughter in her family and had had to work like a man all her life. At five feet eleven she was as tall as her husband, and Frank suspected that, if she took a notion to, she could wring him out like a pair of long drawers. Somehow that made her more appealing to him too.

Mary's expression was inscrutable.
"Well, you two best get goin', then. You'll
be all day a-gettin' there and back as it is.
Paw's expectin' you to watch out for Lee.
Kiss the baby."

Frank sidled his horse close to the
porch and obeyed as Maw Jane stooped
slightly to accommodate him.

"Fine boy you got here," Jane
murmured, her first participation in the
conversation. "He'll grow up to be a good
man. You have a caution, son. I wish
you'd change your mind."

"*Gussssss,*" the baby lisped as his
father's misshapen upper lip touched his
forehead.

At seven months of age, little George had already made a few attempts to talk— so far only Ma-ma, Pop-pop, Paw for Grandpa Fat and Nang for Grandma Jane, but he was quick to pick up on whatever the adults in the house said and now always seemed to be trying his best to frame their words and repeat them. Hen, Jane, Mary, and John all looked at one another, and then at Frank.

Jane shuddered. "Out of the mouths of babes and sucklings," she whispered.

Embarrassed again, Frank coughed and cleared his throat. "I'll take care, Maw. Little George just heard me talkin' was all," he finally replied.

He swung the horse back around to face John, who had smiled at Hen as the older man tried to break the tension with one of his customary tall tales about the virtues of a prize cow he'd acquired down in the low country around Flemingsburg. As usual, though, Hen left out the part about the cow giving bad milk.

"C'mon, John," Frank interrupted, "Lee'll be waitin' on us."

The two waved, turned their mounts, and set off at a brisk trot down the creek.

"Oh, and pick me up a new pipe if you can think of it," Mary, who had smoked since she was nine years old, having acquired the habit from lighting her blind grandmother's pipe, called from the porch as Maw Jane passed baby George to her and took one of the milk buckets.

"Ye see Jim or Lewis or any of their'n up there," yelled Hen as he and Jane stepped off the porch and up the rise to the barn, "tell 'em we said hello!"

Frank and John answered with a wave. Jim Harman was Hen's oldest brother, the man who had laid warrant for the entire Right Fork of Greasy right after the War and had then become a rich man by selling and renting much of the property on it to ex-Confederate soldiers and sympathizers like himself. The residents jokingly called the long hollow and the three below it, Pigeon Roost and the Middle and Buttermilk Forks of Greasy, the Little Confederacy. Run out of Johnson County by postwar Republican threats of vengeance, Jim Harman now lived near his and Hen's oldest half-brother Lewis Mitchell, in solidly and securely Democratic Floyd County not far from the governmental seat of Prestonsburg. Frank liked his uncle Lewis. Like him, Lewis was another family woods colt, and he never gave the boy a rough time about his illegitimate status the way some men did.

The foggy dawn slowly broke into a beautiful spring morning, April 17, 1885,

as Frank Harman and his cousin of sorts
John Addington rode down the right fork
of Greasy Creek and up Pigeon Roost to
meet Mary's next-oldest brother, General
Lee Viers. The three were headed for a
grand festival in Prestonsburg, Kentucky,
the public hanging of Gus Finley for the
murder of Jimmy Hunt.

CHAPTER TWO

I woke up hollering this morning, just like has happened so often. Before I'd finally gotten to sleep I'd had the big eye for hours. A long time after they quit hammering and sawing and finishing up on the gallows past dark last night over near the courthouse, I could still hear the ringing of the hammers and the rasp of the saws in my head. I'm surprised, really, that I dozed off at all. But I won't have the big eye nor wake up that way tonight.

Sol Derossett, the night turnkey here at the jail, came running down the cell corridor like he always does to make sure I've woke up all right, just as if each of my nightmares is some sort of brand-new happening that scares him out of his wits.

Maybe it really does throw that much of a

fright into him. Sol's a good boy; me and

him are the same age, twenty, and we've

even gone swimming at night in the Big

Sandy plus a few other things that the

jailer never heard about or he's decided to

ignore in case he did. Jim Layne's not a

bad sort either, even though he's in county

politics up to his eyeballs. Any jailer is. It's

just that him and Sol's relief shift have got

to help old Jake Hollifield kill me today,

and neither Sol nor Jim seems to know how

to talk to me or do anything for me where

they don't have Death written all over their

faces and through their eyes. I guess I'd act

the same way towards anybody that was

to hang if I was a turnkey or a jailer or a

sheriff or whatever. That is if I'd never been

on this side of the bars myself...

I got up off my corn shuck bed tick,

rubbed my hands up through my hair,

knuckled the sleep seeds out of the corners

of my eyes, and ambled over to the bars

where Sol's face peered in. I hoped it didn't

show in my neck how fast my pulse was

beating, and that my old wool britches

were big and thick enough so Sol couldn't

see how weak and shaky my legs were. I

pulled up the pants and took a big old deep

breath. They won't let a man have a belt or

suspenders in here, which in my case

makes no sense at all. From what I

understand there's supposed to be some

more men assigned in here keeping an eye

on me all the time, but I've not seen any of them since a little before midnight. They're probably off behind the wall, drunk.

"I'm all right," I told him, "just one of them same dreams been a-plaguin' me for seven months now. You and me both should be used to 'em. I'm awake. When Aunt Sally gets here, could you ask her to heat me up a couple pans of water or somethin' so I could bath?"

"Sure, Gus, any old thing you want, you just ask and I'll get it for you," he answered me. I bet he'd like to ask the reason I want to take a bath, though I reckon it's my own business. But the fact is, you can't keep lice off you in a jailhouse and I just don't want to die lousy, nor

43

sweaty nor dirty neither if I can help it. Not

that it really makes any difference, I

reckon...

"Sol?"

He kind of jumped. He was almost

as bad a bundle of nerves as I was.

"What?" he croaked back, like he

half expected me to ask him to take my

place later on.

"I was just curious, was you asleep

out there at the desk when I hollered out?"

He kind of looked shamefaced a

minute, though Lord knows, after some of

the rules he's done broken for my sake in

here, he ought not to be ashamed of any

words we had between each other. "Well, yeah, I was," he answered slowly.

"Ain't you never been afeared I'd figure a way to unlock the cell and sneak outa this place when I caught you a-nappin'?"

"Lord how mercy God, Gus," he replied softly, shaking his head a little. "Don't you know by now how many nights here I've wished you'd done just that, and Jim Layne has too? Why do you think Jim and Sheriff Harris talked to Judge Rice to order you brought back here atter the commonwealth's attorney wanted you took downriver to Catlettsburg? Why'd they make you a trusty out sweepin' the streets, to boot? And I know you give me your word

45

of honor you wouldn't run away that night I took you a-swimmin', but so help me God I wouldn't have minded if you had. You've done had two dozen chances already to head back to the Tug Fork and get right acrost. They ain't nobody here in town wants to see this happen now except Ralph Booten and some of the Hunts and the store owners and Jake Hollifield and his bunch and maybe Judge Rice, though I don't know about him. And well, 'course, that crowd that's comin' into town already, they want for it to happen, which is the reason the shop owners wants it too. The hucksters done got their wagons here and set up too, and before long Jim's gonna have to start juggin' the country boys that the deputies'll bring in because they've *drunk too much too early and started sworpin'. But you, your own self, is the reason why Sheriff Harris quit and why Sheriff May won't have nothin' to do with— this, and why they had to let that old Hollifield in on it. We've give you a chance, son. And you ain't made a move, just like as if you think everything's all right no matter what happens. I don't understand it."*

I nodded my head. It's hard to explain, I know. Maybe I really don't understand it myself. But I tried it one more time.

"Sol, I killed a friend of mine that had never done me no harm. That preys on my mind every single second. I wish to the

*good Lord I'd never took a drink that day,
and never even showed up at that dance. I
wisht I hadn't took my daddy's war stories
about Captain Hatfield over in West
Virginia to heart the way I did. I wish my
mother had lived longer. I wish I'd got a
timber job back on Twelvepole Creek or
Guyandotte instead of comin' over here to
Kentucky to look for the same damn kind of
work I could have done at home. I wisht I'd
never laid eyes on that Colt hog-leg Daddy
give me when he died and I brought with
me. I wish Jimmy hadn't been in the way
where he was. I wish that boy that got the
best of me in the fight, the one I missed,
had knocked me out cold or killed me, one
or the other.*

"I wish I hadn't run my mouth the way a damn drunk will. I wish I had a family in this part of the country big enough to swing a vote in the elections so's the courthouse gang could talk Governor Knott into commutin' my sentence to life in prison. I could live with that as long as I knowed I was payin' my debt. I wish that slick fancy dude lawyer hadn't made me out to be the man that I probably really am—aw, hell, I wish a lot, Sol, and if wishes was horses every beggar'd be ridin'. I don't wanna die, but they's just some damn reason I ain't never been able to run neither. Maybe like it'd foller me no matter what elst I done or wherever I went. And I'm sorry I cussed just now too. Shows how big a sinner I am, I guess."

"Well, good God, Gus, is hang—is this that's about to happen, is it gonna bring Jimmy back?"

I was just about to answer back for him to try to tell that to the Hunts or to that slick fancy Booten, but I heard the big front doors creak and though I jumped a little higher than usual at the sound, I knew it was probably only Aunt Sally come in to bring breakfast to the prisoners—prisoner I should say, since they let everybody else out the past couple of days and it's only me in here this morning. Good thing, too, since me and Sol both knew that this talk was going nowhere, just like all the other times I've tried to tell him what it's like on the inside of my skin.

"I'll see ye later, Gus," Sol mumbled as he went back down the corridor to check on Aunt Sally. I just nodded my head.

I went back to my tick, laid down on my back with my hands underneath my neck, and looked out the barred window into the blue-gray early morning sky. It must not know whether it's Yankee or Confederate, which is sort of like West Virginia and Kentucky both. My heart felt like it was hammering right out of my chest. I didn't really see any point in living once I'd killed a man, but God... God... God... God... I am so afraid to die, to be sent to the place I sent Jimmy Hunt last year.

I've had a lot of time just to lay and look up at the ceiling and through the window and think, but oftentimes my thoughts are so wild I can't even tell Sol nor anybody else about them. But I guess I have the Professor to thank for learning how to figure things out and to put them into order in my mind. Whether that's good or bad I may never know. One part of me can't forget what I've done and wants to atone for it. Another part in there is frighted out of all reason at meeting a just and righteous God, with Jimmy's blood on my head. Then there's yet another part of me that doesn't believe in a thing that he can't touch nor taste nor smell and believes only about half of what he hears and sees, and wonders if there even is a God and if when

I fall through that trap door later today I'll just keep going down into a black hole of nothingness and whatever it was that made up Gus Finley will rot away in the earth. Then the believing part wriggles in there again like a snake, tellin' me for dead certain sure that that just and righteous God will send me to a special little personal hot spot in hell not only for killing Jimmy but for lacking the faith to believe in Him too, which is supposed to be a worse crime than murder.

The only one I think I'd ever trust enough to talk to about things like that is the Professor, though I'd never brought them up to him before and I'm still not sure whether he's a man, an angel, or a devil. I never knew anybody doubted God before,

unless you count him with the questions he

comes up with sometimes, and it can be

hard to figure out exactly what he says he

believes in. Though I went to church all the

time growing up over on Twelvepole across

the Tug and watched them shout and carry

on every meeting weekend, I just never did

think much about God, or life or death

either, one way or the other till all this

happened and I was responsible for

another boy's blood myself.

The preachers here in town have all

been as good to me as they know how to

be. The Baptist and the Presbyterian and

the Methodist and the Campbellite all

started taking turns coming to see me after

I wound up in here. They brought me a nice Bible and a new copy of the Thomas Hymns, and I've had the time on my hands to read and memorize a good many of the hymns as well as a little Bible too. Now that it's gotten close to my execution, at least two of them have been here every day. It all went pretty well between them till about a month ago when the Baptist and the Campbellite finally got around to arguing about maybe baptizing me and what it would do for me, then both of them sort of made up off and on for a while by quarreling with the Methodist and the Presbyterian over the same thing. Then they'd fall out between the two of them again. So they all started trying to keep themselves separated a little bit so I wouldn't hear them quarrel, which would make it out like none of them really know what they're talking about, and which is my main problem. They all claim to believe in the same Bible and all of them think they have the right about what was and what is and what shall be, and yet they can't agree over the only thing that they say that they're led by and that can be depended on. I'd prayed with every lastin' one of them and listened to what each of them told me to do in order to get right. And whether I'd have let the Methodist sprinkle me or the Campbellite wash my sins off in the creek, down deep I knew it wouldn't make any difference because I'm not changed a bit on the inside.

The nightmares have always just made it worse. If it wasn't for the dreams I kept having about the Professor alongside them, I think I'd have done been sent to the insane asylum or hung already for just being a lunatic and a nuisance. A lot of the time it's the same dream repeating itself over and over. The first time I had it was the Sunday night back last fall when the jury finally settled on their verdict and gave it to the judge on Monday. In the dream I think I'm in hell, but I can't say for sure. It's dark, anyway, and it looks like it, but it's kind of chilly rather than hot. I'm in a corner with just enough light barely to make out what's going on in front of me and even then it seems like I'm trying to see through something that's covering up

my face. But then I see the devil. Though he
doesn't have any pitchfork or cloven hooves
or tail, his mouth is all blood red when he
opens it and talks and I know something
like that doesn't belong on a human.
Sometimes he sees me and turns around
the other way and goes back, like he's
scared of me or just doesn't want anything
to do with me. I guess I should be glad of
that. But the worst of the times and in the
most dreams, and how I know he's the
devil more than how he looks, is when he's
beating a little bitty soul to death with what
looks like a harness or a piece of plow
rigging but is probably some castle
dungeon torture thing that I've not seen
before and it just looks like horse rigging. I
can hear the little soul stammer and

scream and beg him for mercy, and all it gets in answer back from the devil is curses and more hits. I try to holler out to the little soul and I want to run over to try to knock the devil away from it and help it, but by then the devil has turned his back to me so he can't see me. I can't hardly breathe to yell at him and I can just barely touch the ground with my toes like I was held up and halfway floating or something and can't get back down, and so I've just got to look on and watch and try to wriggle my feet around and there's not a thing I can do. It ends every time with me screaming and waking up, just like this morning when I scared the socks off Sol again.

I hadn't dreamed about the Professor for several nights, though, and that was one thing I missed. If you could say I had good dreams at all, they were about him, but still I wished I knew who or what he was and why I dreamed so much about him. I don't even know if he's real; I've only met him in my dreams. But unless he's on the other side, if there is another side, I figured I'd spoke my last to him because I didn't see any way that I could get back to sleep again today; not without Jake Hollifield and the boys helping me along to it, anyway.

CHAPTER THREE

It was a long way to Prestonsburg, so Frank and John traveled at a sprightly pace up to the gap at the head of Pigeon where they planned to meet Lee. They'd waved at Uncle Billy Sparks and Richard and Dan, who were out working in what appeared to be an already thoroughly weeded patch of potatoes and sallet peas. The Sparkses had waved back like good neighbors should, but still they'd acted a bit stiff and formal. After he had lowered his hand, tall, gaunt Uncle Billy had bent his head and jammed his hoe, almost hard enough to snap the handle, into the cleaned balk between two potato rows. He swung as if he had seen a copperhead at his feet and was trying to kill it, though it was early in the year and indeed early in the morning for a snake to be active.

"What's the matter'th them?" John asked Frank as he twisted round to face him, his voice vibrating from jouncing up and down roughly on the trotting mule.

"Shh! I'll tell ye atter we get up beyond the Stan'ford place," muttered Frank in return, spurring his old nag a bit harder as they rode past the nearby cabin of Uncle Billy's oldest son Tom. Frank again attempted a neighborly hail to Tom, his wife Mary, and their children, but although neither Tom nor Mary were overtly hostile their five year-old boy, Casandrew, scampered out to the bridle path and threw a few dirt clods at the riders' retreating backs, while his two year-old brother John toddled furiously to keep up with Cas. It did no good for their mother to scold the boys, for they didn't stop, and finally she grabbed a miniscule twig from a nearby tree and hurried after them.

Frank looked back and nearly smiled at Mary Sparks. She was one of the part-Cherokee Baldridges, with raven-black hair and blazing deep blue eyes, from John's Creek. Although Frank was wild about his own Mary, he had to admit that Tom's wife was undoubtedly the most beautiful woman he had ever laid eyes on.

After Frank and John passed Zack Standifer's at the head of the branch, they turned to ride through the gap to Stonecoal and thence to the creek that would one day be popularized in song and story as Butcher Holler. Frank slowed his mount, ready to talk once more. The horse and mule panted a bit from the brisk upgrade trot, and Frank and John knew that they'd have to water both beasts and themselves at Miller's Creek.

"John, I think they was a bit—well, maybe just a little put out with us back there on Pigeon," said Frank, still talking lowly.

"The Sparkses was? Well, I figured the little boy was throwin' clods for some reason. But why?"

"Well you see, Uncle Billy come here from Greenup County. He's got a bunch of kin down that way yet, but they was all Union men and he married Aunt Betty from up in this part of the country and he went with the Confederates like all her people. Course, it didn't help none neither that General Garfield come in here and run Jim Nine Toes Ward and Aunt Betty's brothers and Uncle Billy and a bunch of others all off to prison in Ohio without no bail nor trial for five or six months. He done it just on account of they was suspicioned to be for the South and I reckon old Lincoln made it all legal when he done away with the bail laws. You know the churches couldn't even have assoc'ations 'round here at that time because people was so scared they'd be hauled off to jail just for gatherin' together? Paw Hen and Uncle Jim told me that one time. Anyways, Tom was about twelve at the time and they say Aunt Betty holp him hide inside a foddershock out in the field to keep 'em from takin' him too. That'd make a Confederate outa any man whether he was inclined that way before or not."

"Come to think on it, I've heared that story about the 'soc'ations..."John said, checking his speech quickly with a slight blush. He didn't want to insult Frank and make him mad, and his foster cousin's background of an illegitimate preacher father made any talk around him of Baptists and churches and associations a ticklish subject.

"Anyhow, atter that, Uncle Billy fit for the South, and that's how come him and Aunt Betty moved up here on Greasy and Uncle Jim sold him his place there on Pigeon," Frank continued, apparently not noticing. "But they was a nephew of his down at Ashland, name of Ellis Craft, that got hung a couple of years ago. I forgot and told Dick yesterday what we was gonna do, tryin' to get him to come with us, and I bet they're kindly feelin' bad this mornin' on account of the hangin'. Hain't our fault, though. We didn't kill nobody."

"Well, well. What'd he get hung fer?"

Frank laughed. "What *fer?* Cat fur to make kitten britches!"

"Now Frank, I know you like a joke, but..."

Frank got serious. "I know, I know," he admitted. "I maybe shouldn't of said that. Well, from what the talk was at the time, he was in a gang that was guilty of murder," lowering his youthful voice a bit further to explain, "and...well...rape."

"Jesus Christ!"

"Yeah. It like to of killed Uncle Billy. He worried hisself to death over it. He got to thinkin' he'd brought a curse somehow on the boy because of...well, somethin' that he done durin' the War. Just let Paw Hen tell you about it sometime later if he's ever of a mind to. Uncle Billy's a good man now, and his boy Green that's a preacher over on Daniel's Creek tried and tried to talk him outa that notion, but he wouldn't listen. You'ns was still back over on Little Elk at the time, but I remember when ever'body was talkin' about the Ashland Tragedy. Uncle Billy just walked at a lope up and down Pigeon all the time, with his hands behind his back, right from the mouth all the way up to the head. Ever'body said that Ellis Craft swore up and down right to his dyin' breath, though, that he was innocent."

"Never heared that story atall," John murmured thoughtfully. "This county's a meaner place than I thought it was."

"And then, well, it didn't help Uncle Billy none that his other boy Nelse, you may not remember him, was in jail at the time for stealin' a rope. He didn't get out till about a year atter it all happened."

"Stealin' a *rope?* And went to *jail* fer it? Lord how mercy God, I'm gonna get Poppie and Mom to move back over to Little Elk! This county's dangerous!"

"Well, yeah, he stole a rope. But it woulda gone easier on him iffen it hadn't of had a cow belongin' to Bart Pack tied on the other end of it, though."

John's mirth exploded. "I swear, Frank, you can't be serious 'bout nothin'," he chortled. "Just like Uncle Hen. Well, it does sound like the Packs not to look at nothin' like that as a joke. Poppie said the only time he ever traded with Bart Pack he got to figurin' things up atter it was over, and when all was said and done he'd wound up givin' Bart a calf and payin' him five dollars to take it."

Frank grinned a little. He'd thrown in the anecdote about Nelse Sparks because he felt like he had to get his traveling companion's good mood back after telling the sordid story of the Ashland

Tragedy, and his questionable status in the Harman family was no secret to John. It seemed to him that he always had to be on his toes around the Harmans, to say and do the right things—and some of them always appeared to be on pins and needles around him.

"I 'preciate ye sayin' that about Paw Hen," he rejoined, "But he's a trader too, y'know. C'mon, Lee's a-waitin' for us on the ridge, and we're a-burnin' daylight."

They spurred on up to the ridge that joined Stonecoal and Buffalo Creeks and the Pigeon Roost and Hurricane Forks of Greasy, and found Lee Viers waiting on them, dressed in his best and sitting in high-top boots on a saddle of sorts, makeshifted from a sack of grain doubled and draped on the back of his father's big draft mare. The beast was stamping its hooves and blowing, since its young rider had kept it in a gallop all the way up Hurricane. Lee was the youngest of the party; it appeared he had tried to make himself look more mature by shaving that morning, and doing a teenage boy's typical first job of it. He'd left his own faint little mustache alone but more patches of fuzz remained on his neck and near his ears, and there was a small nick on his chin. And of course, he had to take his share of kidding about it from his brother-in-law.

"Lee, why'nt ye get Wash to show you how to use that shaver?" Frank chuckled, knowing full well that thick-bearded Wash Viers had probably never used such an implement in his life.

Lee took it in good humor. "Why, I wouldn't of let him near my throat with a shaver this mornin'!" he rejoined. "He's in a bad mood already from where Uncle Wes come over from Martin County and started goin' on about the War again, and got him and Maw all mad 'cause he said that both Cinthy Viers and the devil had children named Jeff Davis. Didn't help me and Jack and John none to be named atter Robert E. Lee and Stonewall Jackson and John M. Elliott, neither. Paw just set there and took it like he always does, you know, not sayin' nothin' and tryin' to mind his

manners, but atter Uncle Wes got gone
and I reminded him about us goin' to the
hangin', good Lord! He let me have what
he shoulda told Uncle Wes! Went on and
on about how that poor boy was gonna
hang just 'cause he was drunk and tryin'
to act big the same way me and you do,
and that listenin' to the old soldiers tell
war stories had been the ruination of all of
us. Said the way times was gittin' and the
way we was all actin', hit mighta been you
or me for the rope instead!"

The exuberant teenager paused to
catch his breath, and continued: "But
then he cooled down a little and seemed
like got sad sort of, and said that if you
and me thought that watchin' a boy die

would make bigger men out of us, to go right fer it, but he hoped we come back with more sense than we had when we left."

"Well, fellers, you know, about bein' men," John Addington interjected a little hesitantly. "They say they's a house down on the riverbank at Prestonsburg..." he paused... blushed...and sat back in his saddle as if the horn were suddenly making him uncomfortable. Lee made the same motion with a slight shiver. It was obvious to Frank that both boys had already entertained some thoughts about visiting that house.

Frank had been irked a bit at hearing his father-in-law's words; he respected Wash Viers probably more than the man would ever know, and somehow Wash's seldom-voiced anger and ridicule cut deeper than blustery, comical Henderson Harman's possibly could. But John's comment, and his and Lee's obvious condition, gave him the occasion to shrug off his uncertainty with another jest.

"Yeah, you'ns is soldiers now, huh," he laughed, "all standin' at attention and ever'thing. You best stay away from that place. You ain't got the money no way, and even if ye did, all ye'd be payin' for is a case of the pock or the clap." He spurred his old nag. "C'mon, let's git!" he called back over his shoulder.

John and Lee made no more suggestions about that special house on the riverbank. They knew Frank was right; though both of them had been on the worst ends of his sarcasms and his temper tantrums before, his status in their eyes as an old married man merited their respect.

CHAPTER FOUR

Parade rest!

At ease!

As you were!

*Oh, for God's sake, stand down! You
never heeded me before, but why today of
all days won't you pay attention just once?*

*There was no help for it. It was there,
and it was there to stay for a while. All it
must have heard out of what I said to it
was the word* attention, *and it was bound
and determined to stand at that no matter
what order I gave it. I guess I could blame
the whole thing on Aunt Sally's girl Vina
and actually partway on what Aunt Sally*

done herself, but I know it's just as much my own fault as it could be either of theirs. For some reason Vina came to the jailhouse this morning, I reckon to help Aunt Sally out though Vina's never been so work-brittle when there's been a houseful in here rather than just me by myself. She's talked to me through the bars before, though, and once or twice I winked at her and grinned and she blushed and giggled back. She's plumb fetching, for all that she's only fifteen. Aunt Sally likely put the cooker with my breakfast food in it and my tin cup of coffee on the little potbellied stove out front to reheat, and the girl must have got the key out of Sol's coat pocket and brought the food back here to me by herself while Aunt Sally's and Sol's backs were turned. Well, I always have been a fool for a shapely

ankle, but good God. I'd love to have all the

time in the world to think about girls, but of

all the mornings I didn't need to, this was

the one. I've never been with a woman in a

private way in my life, for all that a lot of

boys has done married by the time they

reach my age, and I don't know which is

the worst ache, the desire for it or the

curiosity about it. So here was pretty little

yellow-headed Vina right in my cell alone

with me, setting down breakfast and coffee

on my bench and giggling and complaining

about an itch on her ankle that she said

she didn't know whether it was a bug bite

or poison ivy. She leaned forward right in

front of where I sat and pulled up her dress

at the side over her ankle for me to take a

look at it and tell her what I thought it was,
and right then Aunt Sally came storming in
like the wrath of God with Sol right behind
her. The old woman rared back with her
hand and gave that girl the loudest whack
right on her seat that I ever heard. These
jail walls really make an echo. Vina
squealed bloody murder and then giggled
again and jumped backwards rubbing
herself back there and wiggled and run out
of the cell and back down the hall, still
rubbing and wiggling and giggling, all
while Aunt Sally was still scolding her for
showing me her ankle. Aunt Sally was too
irked to think that she might not ought to
have given Vina that swat right while I was
there so close, but any schoolboy can tell
you that seeing something like that, on top

of getting a peek at a pretty ankle already,
only makes a bad matter worse. I didn't
see any bug bite or poison ivy on the ankle,
either.

I felt sorry for poor old Aunt Sally.
She always has been good to me, and truth
to tell I thought she'd blame me for
compromising Vina, like any upstanding
mother would. But after all the peeking and
smacking and squealing and giggling and
wiggling and rubbing and running was
done and over with she put her face in her
hands and cried out loud right in front of
me. Sol just patted her on the shoulder and
tried to tell her there was no harm done,
and I would have done so myself if I'd
dared to stand up right then.

"Gus, honey, I'm so sorry," she kept sobbing over and over again. "That girl's a-turnin' bad on me and I don't know how to keep her from it a-livin' here in this town. I've give in to her just too much since her daddy died and I've took the job as the jailhouse cook, and now I'm a-payin' the price for it. Oh, God forgive me, that was just plumb mean of her to treat you like that, Gus, but she's too young to know, honey. She just didn't know."

Sol rolled his eyes at me, but didn't say anything. I had to grin a little bit back to him. I've talked to him so much I can read his thoughts, and right then he was probably thinking that Vina wasn't as innocent as she was just plain young. But as crazy as it sounds, I wouldn't have missed that show for the world, even if I couldn't do a thing about it. As Aunt Sally swiped at her eyes with her apron I opened my breakfast cooker and started trying to get a few bites down me, before I got to thinking and my stomach went all dauncy on me again. I still couldn't stand up, anyway.

She'd fixed me a bigger breakfast than usual, side meat and fried bread with milk gravy and some canned tomatoes just like I'd asked for my last meal, and I made a show of being hungrier than I was in the hope it might make her feel better. Sol was still waiting on the day turnkeys to get here, so I offered him a bate of it because I knew I couldn't keep much on my stomach, but he said he wasn't hungry. I remember the time back when I was a little boy that everybody in the hills thought tomatoes were poison. Today I almost wish they really were, though I wouldn't tell Sol and Aunt Sally that. I love tomatoes, so I'd just die happy.

Aunt Sally went on back down the hall, sniffling and hollering for Vina again, but I couldn't hear anything that the girl said, or giggled, in return. When I'd swallowed the little bit of food I could and gave Sol the cooker and tin cup back he turned to go. As he stepped outside the cell door and locked it he whispered, "Now Gus, that bathwater hain't warmed up yet.

Would you rather I brought it back here as is, so you can take you a cold bath instead?"

I must have blushed pretty red. "Yep, that'd be a good idea right about now," I murmured.

He nodded. "Some of the church people is supposed to be by sometime this morning with a new suit and shoes they got you, too," he added. "I'll go get your water, and you go ahead and bath and I'll stay right at the end of the hall and make sure Aunt Sally nor Vina don't stray back here and see you. And Gus—well, I'm just sorry that little strollop got you all het up and bothered this morning. Her itchy place is considerable further up on her than her ankle, I'd reckon."

He meant well by saying that, but it bothered me and I could feel my face heat up again. Maybe it wouldn't have if it was any other day, but I was actually still kind of feeling grateful to pretty little Vina and she probably gave Sol some ideas on his own anyway.

"Hain't it about time you got along home to bed anyways?" I asked him. "Jim Layne and the day turnkeys are bound to be here any minute."

I saw him look down. "Who can sleep in Prestonsburg today?" he muttered softly.

"Oh. Well, that means you've got it planned to watch, I guess. I may see you out there, then, before they cover my eyes up."

He took off like a scalded cat after I said that, and I got to feeling bad all over again because if there's been a boy that's tried to be a friend to me since I've been in jail, Sol Derossett has. And to give him credit where credit's due, he did bring my bathwater back to me right then, though he didn't look at me or say anything else. But we never got to say goodbye either, and I wish we could have.

Why is it, I wonder, that a man that's—that's—well, in a hard spot like me this morning, feels down deep in his soul *that he can just live forever, and it's*

nothing but that hot humor he's got that's

making a fool out of him? Are my brains in

the wrong head, or what? I don't know;

maybe that inclination gets worse when

you know you're going to die, though Lord

knows I've had a rough enough time with it

ever since I got the first hair between my

legs. My father told me that once during the

War he was detailed as part of a firing

squad to execute two young boys in his

company that deserted but was caught.

Him and another soldier went to get them

out of the little woodshed that their outfit

had commandeered as a guardhouse, and

both of the boys was kneeling down in

there, their backs to the door, and—well, I

don't even want to think about how he said

they were trying to put in their last

moments except to keep reminding myself

that I hope I've got a little more pride and

decency than to resort to something like

that right now. Daddy said that him and

the other guard was almost tempted to

shoot them both in the back of the head

and let on that they'd tried to escape,

rather than to let them die with that kind of

shame on their heads—not to mention their

hands—before the whole company. Maybe

I should have asked the Professor about

things like that, why is it that men and

boys are made that way, when I had the

chance, but then again maybe not. The

Professor never seemed like the sort of man

you could talk to about such matters, which

is one of the reasons I've wondered so

often if he was an angel coming to me in my dreams.

The harsh lye soap stung my eyes and my scalp both, but in a strange way it felt good. It's not true what they say about a cold bath, though. At least for me it wasn't. I knew unless I aimed to make a laughingstock out of myself later on I'd better get my mind on something else, even if there was a part of my body telling my brain that I was just having another bad dream right then and I'd wake up soon and live forever and beget and beget and beget and beget and have a big grin on my face all for all the pretty girls I'll do that wonderful begetting on. It was so odd, like my flesh had tried to trade off my fear for this crazy wild good feeling, and then it didn't want to give the good feeling up to go back to the fear. I couldn't really say I blamed it. Still, I knew that the fear was only one heartbeat away.

As I finished up and dried my hair and my body I tried to think up the stories and the poems that the Professor had read and some of his talk to me, and call them back to my memory. It was hard, since I never did have all that much schooling unless you count what he's given to me. But that's where I always met him in my dreams: a schoolhouse on a windy day almost like March, which is odd because schools only keep between July after the

*corn is laid by and December when the
hard freezes hit.*

*I remember having the very first
Professor dream back last September right
after I got back to sleep from the first bad
devil nightmare. I don't know how I got to
the school. I just found myself there, the
only scholar, and he was up front, dignified
looking and dressed in a dark suit and a
vest and a necktie and a white shirt with a
high stiff collar, reading very slow and
carefully from a book in a loud, rich deep
voice like he was trying to make a houseful
of noisy little ones pay attention to him. He
looked maybe thirty-nine or forty years old,
but it was strange; in some of the dreams
later on he was younger and in others he*

was a lot older, as if he could change his age and his looks and the time at his own will. For a while, I can't say exactly how long, I just listened to him read and stayed quiet. But finally I tried to interrupt him to ask who he was, where he came from, was he an angel or devil or what, and why was he doing this.

He put his book down, ran his hand over his head—he's not far from being bald no matter what age he is, young or old, which don't seem quite right if he's an angel though I do recollect that one old prophet back there somewhere was bald headed and real ill-tempered to boot—and he looked out at me from under the craggiest eyebrows I ever saw in my life. It was a plumb scary look if you ask me, one that I guarantee could freeze a rattlesnake in mid-strike. It made me think again that he was some kind of devil.

"Augustus Finley," he finally answered me just as slow and deliberate as he'd been reading, "You are to raise your hand and snap your fingers lightly if you need to call my attention to something. There's no need for us not to use good manners. But you need to know that I am neither angel nor devil, just a human being that is quite as imperfect as most humans are."

I must have gaped. Nobody ever called me by my real name, not even my parents most of the time. I was even

arrested, arraigned, tried, and sentenced in
the Floyd County court as Gus rather than
Augustus. I didn't see how he could have
known, although it seemed to me that he
was using my full name as a sign of
respect.

"Are you sure you ain't an angel or a
devil?" I asked. "Excuse me, sir, but
nobody hardly even knows what my real
name is. Seems to me only an angel could
have guessed it."

He looked off out one of the windows
for a second and his eyes were far away.
The windowpanes rattled a little with a
strong gust of wind, another unusual thing
because no schoolhouse I've ever been in
has had glass windows, only shutters.

"March weather," he murmured. "I remember the month of March vividly from my younger days. Well, angels and devils and humans... the difference between them is a long story, Augustus, but one day you—and I—might figure it out. Perhaps that's why we're together in this classroom now."

I just stared. "Mister," I told him, "I don't know the least thing you're talking about. I don't understand at all."

"Neither do I, Augustus, neither do I. Life is not a fair proposition. Anyone who goes through it looking for all the equations to balance out is bound to be disappointed. But I've said enough about that, at least for now. What's done is done, though either of us might be willing to sacrifice our lives so that some things might have turned out differently. You are a dreamer, Augustus, and I am also. I have always had vivid dreams and nightmares myself, and so you might say that I understand you. But so you may know, I am a teacher, and you may call me Professor like most of the people who know me do."

He lowered his head and made out like he was going to start reading another poem and I came in a hair of interrupting him again, but I caught myself and raised my hand and snapped my fingers lightly. He looked up, and this time his eyebrows weren't quite so craggy.

"Yes, Augustus?"

"Sir—Professor, I'm sorry, but could you try to run it by me just one more time why it is that you're here? I 'preciate the poems and the reading and all. I never had a man do that for me before. But I just wish I could get a handle on what's going on here."

He seemed to stop and think; for a minute he gripped his chin in his right thumb and forefinger, and I could see that his right hand was as rough and callused and cracked as both of mine are, or were back when I was working in the timber. Then he answered, in that same voice that was so slow I could almost guess what his next word would be before he finally out with it.

*"There are many things, Augustus, that neither you nor I, nor anyone else, will ever comprehend. I learned that a long, long time ago, and though I've often hated it, I have had to accept it. My best answer to you is this: I am here because I feel that I owe you a great debt. I suspect that I could not speak without you. I doubt that I could even **be** if it were not for you. Why am I here, and not an angel, or a better and more knowledgeable human? I can't even grasp that, much less be at peace about it. But you are here now, and I am here for you."*

"But who am I here for?"

That was the only time I ever woke up from a Professor dream shouting. Sol told me later on that I was hollering out:

But who am I here for? Who am I here

for? Who am I here for? *...until he*

opened the cell door and shook me awake.

CHAPTER FIVE

The journey up hills and down
hollows through left and right Miller's
Creeks, Oaklog and Daniel's Creeks,
across and down John's Creek to its
mouth and then up Big Sandy to
Prestonsburg was tedious. All along the
way Frank, John, and Lee found their
party steadily augmented with other riders
all going in the same direction—mostly
men and boys, as well as a few women
and girls. Lee and John, of course, became
very gallant in the presence of the
unmarried females, making Frank feel all
that much more mature. It had been
Henderson Harman, upriver on a cattle
trip when the killing had occurred who

had first brought the news of the Finley case back to upper Greasy; on the road to Prestonsburg talk about the hanging again flowed freely, and Frank, John, and Lee gradually pieced together Gus Finley's entire story from the combination of rumors.

Gus wasn't even of legal age yet, only a year older than Frank and John. Back twelve months or so ago near the mouth of Mud Creek in upper Floyd County, he and a bunch of his friends had gotten drunk at a dance and he'd gotten into a fight with one of them, John Degley. Degley had bested him and walked away, but Gus wasn't willing to leave matters alone; like so many mountain boys who'd grown up hearing war stories from their veteran fathers were now doing as a matter of habit, Gus was packing a revolver in his pocket, and he'd staggered up from the ground and drawn it. Trouble was, he was so badly mauled and still so drunk that he couldn't see straight, and he'd mistakenly killed another boy, seventeen year-old Jimmy Hunt. Thoroughly sobered, his chums had screeched at him that he'd shot the wrong man.

Yet in a near stupor, Gus had just mumbled drunkenly, "Gus will shoot."

Those three words, just as those a writer a continent away and a generation in the future would one-day pen to describe a similar occurrence, became three fateful knocks upon the door of his undoing.

Actually, during his trial for capital murder, support had been high for Gus in eastern Johnson County. This was mainly because Harmon Harris, Uncle Will Ward's son-in-law from down on Banjo Creek who'd had the chance to read law under an older attorney, been admitted to the bar, and made something of himself, had served as the boy's defense counsel. It was a clear case of manslaughter and worthy of a penal sentence, Harmon Harris admitted, for the young man had premeditated nothing against Jimmy Hunt, and had harbored no malicious indifference to the boy's life. He'd killed Jimmy, sure enough, but in a drunken accident, and he was willing to serve the time he merited even if the court handed down a sentence of life imprisonment. It simply wasn't a hanging case. Only seven years before in Floyd County, David Thornsbury had killed Samuel Gray in what all the eastern Kentucky newspapers had admitted was a family feud; worse than that, at around the same time at Whitesburg, up near the head of the North Fork of the Kentucky River several miles south of Prestonsburg, Charles Trusty had been arrested and jailed for kicking his sick grandchild to death. Neither man had received a capital sentence, however much justice might have miscarried at least in the latter case. Gus Finley certainly deserved the same clemency.

But at Gus's trial eloquent state's attorney Ralph Booten, knowing that a successful capital prosecution would be a real political feather in his cap, had kept hammering away at the jury of Floyd County farmers and small businessmen with those three fateful words: **Gus will shoot, Gus will shoot, Gus will shoot**. Whether from Booten's golden oratory and his urgings that Floyd County needed to make an example of a murderer, the fact that the number of violent crimes in the hills was steadily and frighteningly increasing, or the reality that Gus Finley simply didn't have the all-important local family voting connections to make either a lighter sentence or a pardon a political reality, the twelve men had returned a guilty verdict and judgment of death to Circuit Judge John M. Rice on September 16, 1884. That was one day Frank could remember well; it was a Monday, and baby George had been born in Wash and Cynthia Viers' little cabin on Hurricane on the hot, sultry afternoon before. He had a feeling that he would savor the memory of this April day too.

The sun was high when the steadily growing party reached Prestonsburg. Frank had never seen anything like it; people were streaming in from all directions on horses and mules, in wagons and buggies, and on foot, as if the whole world had stopped and all its inhabitants were congregating in this one little town to watch a boy die. As he, John, and Lee approached the outskirts of the county seat on the riverbank path, their horses jostled with those of the others and piles of droppings littered the rutted dirt road.

"You know," Frank said to his companions as they tried to avoid the press and the muck simultaneously, "I bet we can't even ride in close to the hangin'. We're gonna have to leave these horses somewhere back here and walk on in if we're gonna watch."

"Well, this is a town, Frank," John replied as he reined in his mule closer.

"You don't reckon somebody'd try to steal 'em?"

Frank laughed. "Who'd want to steal this old plug, or your old mule? Lee's, though, I mean Wash's, now, that's another matter. I hate to have to go to a livery stable, though, us just bein' in town this one day. Aw, I don't know, we'll think of somethin'."

Lee remained silent during the exchange, with a distant look on his face and kept swallowing frequently.

Unused to town sights as they were, the booming voice a few yards away from them startled the trio: "Well, boys, just how far behind *is* the law atter ye?"

"Uncle Jim, it's good to see ye!" exclaimed John, as he and Frank turned their mounts in the direction of the voice. Lee sat his horse silently as if he had not heard anything. His eyes were somewhere in the distance, as if he had caught sight of the gallows this far back from the center of town.

Big Jim Harman rode up to his nephew and foster nephew with friendly eyes, but a serious countenance. As always when he saw one of Hen's brothers, Frank wondered a moment at the contrasts between the Harman men. James, the oldest, was tall, heavy, thick-bearded, broad-shouldered, and muscular, like Wash Viers; Willie, who'd gone Republican and Union with his wife's people in the War, was clean-shaven and thinner; and Hen, the youngest, short, roly-poly, and sparse-bearded, was said to be the spit and image of their Dutch father. Most of Willie and Jim's boys, though, had Jim's heavy build, and Frank wondered what he would have looked like if he were Hen and Jane's own son. At least he probably wouldn't have this lip, he mused as he bit at his scraggly mustache.

"I don't reckon your folks come with ye, did they? Is Green and Angie and their'n here?" Big Jim asked, naming his one remaining daughter and son-in-law still living back on upper Greasy. Frank, intimidated a bit by his ambivalent status in the Harman family, let John do the talking.

"No sir," John answered with a smile, "it's just us from up in the Little Confederacy this mornin'. Green and Angie are well, though. Don't know if any of Uncle Willie's is here or not. Didn't see none of 'em out over on Daniel's Creek. How's Aunt Polly and Uncle Lewis and ever'body?"

Uncle Jim nodded his head. "They're well, thank ye. Polly's back up home and I reckon Lewis is too ...at his place. Ain't seen him today. Allen and Brownlow and Richard's all here with some of Lewis's boys and grandboys, though, and I cain't get none of the durn fools outa town. I just rode up this way to see if I could see anybody from Johnson, and it looks like the whole durn country's out. I'm glad that Hen and Jane and Green and Angie and Shade and Hanner didn't come, though. Even Willie musta done somethin' right for once. Looks like some of my family has got walkin'-around sense atter all..."

Frank lowered his head and looked back around at Lee, now even more content to let John carry on this conversation. It sounded just a little too familiar for him to venture a word.

"Why, Uncle Jim, what's the matter?" asked John, a bit taken aback himself.

Jim Harman scowled fiercely. *"Ever'thing's* the matter, Johnny Morgan," he growled, using John Addington's middle name, as was his habit. General John Hunt Morgan had been one of Jim's heroes twenty-odd years before, and little sawed-off Hen had actually ridden with the famous Confederate raider for a brief time back in the 'sixties. Frank had heard Maw Jane tell the story many times of how she had had to go all the way to Campbellsville at war's end to help get Hen released from Federal custody, and how the two of them had married there before journeying back east, home to Greasy Creek.

"You listen here, boys," Jim continued. "This thing is wrong from the get-go. I know ever'body was wantin' to see that boy hung last year right atter the killin', but this ain't justice. Finley's been a trusty here at the jail for months, out cleanin' the streets and ever'thing, and you won't find no better boy. He's never said a bad word nor done a wrong turn to nobody since they brought him in, and he's never once offered to run. Sweet Jesus, that Derossett boy that's the night turnkey over there has even took him swimmin' in Big Sandy atter midnight and he didn't try to get away!"

Big Jim paused, his eyes misting and drifting a bit. He continued more softly: "Two boys, swimmin' and splashin' and duckin' one another and talkin' about girls under the full moon, all fulla piss and vinegar and life the way that boys ort to be, that turnkey and Finley together. And that turnkey is gonna live to be an old man, Ralph Booten's figurin' to use this as a ticket to Frankfort, and today Gus Finley's gonna die 'cause Governor Knott won't hear nothin' about a pardon. He'll pardon them durn fools a-fightin' all over Breathitt County if the juries over there don't acquit 'em outright, for what reason God knows if they ain't a-bribin' him or less'n he thinks they can swing the vote for him where they live, but he won't show no mercy to Finley. I won't have no part of it. I seen enough dyin' back before you was born. I'm gettin' outa this crazy place as fast as I can git, and you boys better do the same thing."

John swallowed and looked down before answering this time; both he and Frank were now thoroughly disconcerted. John searched haltingly for a reply, mumbling something incoherent about big events, murders, victims, and the law, but Jim Harman cut him short.

"Listen, Johnny Morgan," he said harshly. "W. R. Harris has resigned his office as high-sheriff up here for no other reason than he refused to hang this boy. How many county sheriffs you ever know of that wasn't crooked as a dog's hind leg, and rich from all that they can skim off property taxes with nobody the wiser? And here he give all that up!... All because he felt so strong about this. And Bascom May, the one they put in to replace him, wouldn't even take the job less'n he was promised he wouldn't have to pull the lever on the trap door hisself. So they got this feller Jake Hollifield, some no-account that knowed or was kin or somethin' to the Hunt boy, I don't know, to serve as special deputy in charge of the hangin' and to take care of all of it hisself"—Jim spat in the dust in disgust—"and I know in reason he don't know no more about the job than a cow would. Just took it to make hisself look like a big tough man, I'd bet. And you got to do a hangin' just right, too. Gotta have the knot just so, under the right ear, if you want it to be a mercy death, and you gotta be able to tell just how far he'll have to drop for it to work. Me and Willie rode clean to Morgan County back in the 'fifties to watch Bill Brown hang for killin' the Irish peddler, and I ain't never forgot it. If Hollifield don't get it right—well—" Jim swallowed noticeably and hesitated uncomfortably, his eyes shifting. Lee Viers, his horse still turned in the other direction, shuddered involuntarily.

"What, Uncle Jim?" John murmured, afraid to hear the answer. He and his two companions already knew anyway.

"Let's just say it'll be a good thing that Gus Finley'll have his face covered up," the older man returned. "Hell of a lot of benefit that'll be for *him*, though. I got to go, boys, and I advise you to do the same. This is the devil's town today; the Lord's done packed up and left the place to itself. And us."

A great shout arose from the center of town, and Big Jim swore harshly as he jerked his head toward the sound of the tumult.

CHAPTER SIX

"Yes, Augustus?"

I'd just raised my hand and snapped my fingers. "Professor," I asked him, "I'm sorry but—could you tell me the name again of the piece you just got done readin' to me? I hate to say so but I clean forgot it."

His eyebrows cragged a second, then eased back down again like he'd had a thought that held him back from scolding me for forgetting. He was an old, old man today. The little bit of hair around his temples and the back of his head was almost white, and though his voice was

*just as deep and strong as ever, there was
a sort of rougher, hoarser edge to it.*

*"Certainly, Augustus," he answered.
"It was **Thanatopsis** by William Cullen
Bryant."*

"Thana—what?"

*"Thanatopsis… It's a Greek word,
and it means a view of death. Though
William Cullen Bryant lived to an advanced
age, he was in poor health in his youth and
he brooded much over the prospect of his
decease. He wrote this poem when he was
a young man, and to me at least it shows a
maturity of thought that is remarkable."*

*"I can see that," I replied. "How the
business about living your life so at the end*

of it you lay down gladly, as if you knowed what was waiting on you could be a peaceful sleep and pleasant dreams. But I guess this means, you know, I'm gonna be executed. I thought about askin' you about that the last few times, when you were readin' out of the plays about to be or not to be and be absolute for death and the evil that men do lives after them but the good is oft interried with their bones."

He nodded his head and held his chin in his forefinger and thumb like I've seen him do every time he thinks about something.

"Yes, Augustus," he said finally, "it's a fact, and for whatever it may be worth to you, I want to tell you that I am truly sorry

for it. You don't deserve it, but we all
endure things that we do not deserve, some
more, some less. I don't know why
salvation for some means condemnation for
others. In my life I've known genuine
murderers never even to be accused, or if
they were, to be able to call on their family
connections to sway the law in their favor.
But you have no connections in this part of
the country to depend upon, and in a way
neither do I."

He looked down before he went on
with his speech: "I had a son that was shot
in cold blood near the head of the creek on
which I have lived almost my entire life. His
killer got two years in the penitentiary for
second-degree manslaughter because he

had a lawyer uncle who knew how to work Kentucky's judicial system in a way that my family connections would never have allowed me. In the courtroom that lawyer called my boy a potential criminal of long standing, and he was able to get away with it. Though my son was full of mischief, he was no criminal, and Augustus—my students all know I have a strong temper and they dread my scoldings, but I had always been able to keep my wrath under control until that day at the trial. I don't remember much after the lawyer made that statement, but the four men it took to wrestle me out of the courtroom told me later that I climbed over chairs and tables trying to reach him, roaring, 'You lie! You lie on my dead boy!'"

The Professor shook his head then murmured softly, "That is one of the few times in my life that I have genuinely wanted to do bodily harm to anyone, but it would not have brought my son back to me if I had succeeded. For the rest of his life that lawyer studiously avoided me. If he saw me in town, he would cross the street as fast as he could to get away from me. I have never told a student of these things before, Augustus, but yours is a special case. I've mentioned to you already that life is not fair at all."

I hung my head and felt my cheeks burn. "Professor—I'm really sorry about your son, sir," I muttered. "He sounds just like me almost, and truth be told, he sounds just like the boy I killed, too. Jimmy didn't deserve what he got from me and I may never forgive myself. I'm just as guilty as the man who shot your son, I guess. I don't know why you're even giving me the time of day."

"Unfairness works both ways, Augustus," he replied. "You're a young man. It is only natural for the young to want to hold on to life, and my son's killer was no different in that respect than any other boy his age. He simply had the advantage of his family connections and could employ it. But on the other side of the coin, so to speak—do you think you'll be the youngest person ever to be hanged in Kentucky?"

"I—I don't know, Professor. Never thought about it that much, I guess."

"You won't be," he answered. "That distinction, dubious as it is, goes to a twelve year-old boy named Bill James, who was hanged near Versailles in Woodford County in 1791 for murder. Do you really think a twelve year-old boy is capable of the crime of murder, in the premeditated way that an adult could be? I've often wondered what pretext the citizens of Woodford County used to acquit their own conduct in that matter."

I thought for a moment. "Well, sir," I said, "that was back in the frontier times, when men had to be a lot rougher. Who really knows? Could he have been an

Indian boy maybe who'd tomahawked and scalped a white family?"

The Professor's eyebrows cragged. "Who knows indeed, Augustus?" he growled bitterly. "But Bill James wasn't an Indian. He was black. A slave, with none of the powerful family connections that made dueling, which was often the same as murder, a so-called affair of honor among his so-called betters. And if you happen to maintain the illusion that we Kentuckians of more modern times can be any more civilized when we smell blood, especially that of a creature weaker than we are, then let me tell you about a hanging that took place near New Castle in Henry County, on the lower Ohio River not too far from

Louisville. I'd say it happened a few years

after you were born. A thirteen year-old ex-

slave named Susan, a poor girl who made

her living as a babysitter for white folk,

was convicted of murdering one of the

children in her care. Augustus, my wife and

I found one of our daughters, only a month

old, dead in her crib one morning. Do you

think that Susan could have been accused

of such a dreadful crime simply because

one of her charges died of unexplainable

causes, just like ours did? Or perhaps from

an accident that no one could have

foreseen? But anyway—Susan was

hanged on February 7, 1868, and the

newspapers of the day reported that the

rope was cut up into short pieces

afterwards because so many of the

upstanding citizens who witnessed the deed, requested souvenirs."

The Professor looked away and held his chin again. "Man's inhumanity to man makes countless thousands mourn," he murmured softly. "Robert Burns was so right."

I had to think about that one another minute. All of a sudden the world seemed even more unfair to me than it had even for the past year. I don't know how to explain it, but somehow his telling me about those two children gave me courage. I felt sorry for little Bill and Susan, but if they'd had to go through what they did, I reckoned I could some way too. If I just had a way to know, I could be brave. I told the Professor

that, too, and though he didn't answer, he
did give me a solemn nod. I figured that he
was open to more questions, so I just
plugged right on.

"Begging your pardon, Professor," I
asked, "have you ever been in my shoes
before? Thought you yourself was going to
die, or have you been pulling my leg all this
time and you are an angel or a devil one or
the other?"

He grinned sort of wryly all of a
sudden like I'd just said something funny
and cheered him up a bit, but he sobered
his face back down fast.

"Augustus, if you recall, during our
very first conversation you asked me about

the devil," he replied quietly. "So let me turn the question back to you now: do you believe in a personal devil? A divinely-created higher being with the power, or at least the nature, of a malevolent angel whose sole purpose is the temptation and destruction of mankind?"

"Well, I reckon so. There's God and the devil both, aren't they?"

"God is another matter. But as to the personification of temptation, ruin, and destruction, are you really sure that mankind needs any extra help or resources than it already has at its own disposal? Does the devil tempt humans, or do humans become devils by getting lazy or complacent and giving way to a set of general defects that we all harbor? Who was in charge of the hangings I just told you about? God, the devil, or man? Don't answer that; I only want you to think about it. But—yes, once in my lifetime I thought I was going to be murdered. I survived, though."

"Excuse me, Professor, I know it's forward to ask, but—why did you think you was going to be killed? Who was the man who tried to kill you?"

He held his chin with his thumb and finger a long time after that and looked away, like he was really having a harder time than usual putting his words together. Finally, he answered me.

"It was a man, Augustus, for whom I held both love and terror at first. Later on, if I called up some memories and didn't think of others, I found that I could easily harbor little but hatred for him. But even later than that, I came to see him as a product of his environment—what he became as a man was, in a large sense, shaped by the circumstances of his birth and some of the things he had endured as a small child. After I knew that, I couldn't hate him any more, or at least I could try to refuse to think of the injustices he had done me. But I must credit him with this. He gave me an appreciation of the profession of teaching that I couldn't have acquired anywhere else. I've worked at much in my life, ever since I was old enough to work and, if truth

137

be told, some of it when I was actually too young to work. I've farmed, raised cattle and hogs, cut timber, helped dig and repair dirt roads, and weighed coal. But none of that mattered like the day I became a teacher when I was seventeen years old. In our mountains, teaching is one of the few professions that allow one to spend any time reading, and I always loved books—so I told myself that reading was the primary advantage of being a schoolmaster. Still, through my—assailant, shall we say, I was able to see that what happens to the child often warps the adult, and I knew that the guidance and the example of a good teacher is one means by which the life of such a child might be turned around. I can't say that this type of change happens always. Perhaps it does not even occur often. But if there is only one bare chance that it might be brought about, it's worth a lifetime of effort to make that one chance happen."

He paused a second longer than usual. "Not everyone who is acquainted with me thinks I am quite as religiously orthodox as I should be," he concluded. "My own mother once asked me if I was willing to admit that God made man. But I know beyond the shadow of a doubt that the privilege of teaching can be a holy thing, and I thank God every day that I have been allowed to be a teacher. For this reason I thank you too, Augustus."

Today the Professor was making the longest speeches I'd ever heard out of him, apart from reading a long poem or something, and as slow as he always spoke it took him forever to say all of it. But I was still full of questions.

"Professor?"

"Go ahead, Augustus."

"What's waitin' on me beyond the grave? You said you thanked God every day. Do you mean that you do it in person? Have you been there too, and can you tell me about God like the preachers try to do?"

"You certainly are asking the difficult ones today, Augustus," he replied as his eyes got another faraway look. "But then

again," he continued, "I've just told you a few things not quite compatible with polite sitting-room conversation myself. Old Job, in the Bible, put forth the question to his three friends: if a man die, shall he live again? Let me ask you something else. Which would you prefer, given the choice between two things: the existence of God but no life after death, as it appears that the ancient Sadducees believed, or the nonexistence of God but the guarantee that your own existence will continue in a hopeful, if not happy, state beyond death?"

"What?"

"That's another question you needn't bother trying to answer, Augustus. And certainly it's not one I've ever asked a *student before, or ever expect to ask again.*

It's just food for thought. Most people had

rather not even consider questions like that.

The ideas of God and immortality are

inextricably bound up with one another,

within our own souls if nowhere else. But

yes, I believe that there is a Divinity to

which you and I can aspire to worship, and

that our highest expressions of worship are

to seek the truth both within and outside

ourselves, wherever and however we might

find it. I believe to use that truth to make a

positive difference in the world in which we

*live is what makes **any** difference there is.*

And as for immortality, can you, I, or

anyone else claim to know the limits and

bounds either of love, or of human creative

consciousness? As King Solomon, who is

supposed to have been the wisest of all men, said once, love is as strong as death."

"I still don't understand, Professor. Which preacher should I listen to, then? I've got four coming to see me and they're trying their best not to fall out with one another for fear of giving an offense and making me lose my soul, but I still don't know which one of 'em to put full trust in. If any..."

"You should listen to them all, Augustus. And listen to none of them so closely that you accept what any of them say on mere blind trust, or because you have let your mind become so lazy that swallowing a predigested set of ideas or beliefs appears to be the easiest course of *action. I never tried to preach, but I always*

wondered whether I could have or not. And

I have known, or known of, a few

preachers that were blatant hypocrites—

some in my own family, even. But for all

their faults, the great many of them are

mostly honest folk, sometimes happy,

sometimes unhappy, often confused and

often honestly mistaken, and frequently

angrier than they'd ever admit because

they are secretly unhappy and confused

and suspect that they are mistaken. They

blame these feelings on the devil, then they

fight their perception of this devil and if

they are not careful they wind up looking

exactly like the image with which they

make war. But by and large they try their

best, just as you and I do, to find a glimmer

going to read from. I didn't see how he

could take any pleasure from it, and though

maybe I should, there was no way that I

could either. But he'd been so nice to me to

talk and read to me like this since I've been

here, I couldn't turn him down, so I

swallowed and answered, go ahead.

He nodded at me, but then he did

another thing he'd never done before. He

walked from behind his desk over to me

and grasped my right hand in his own grip,

and shook it hard. "Goodbye for now,

Augustus Finley," he said with a lot of

emotion in his voice. "Again I must tell you

the very truth of my conscience: I could not

*speak without you. I could not **be** without*

you. Thank you from the bottom of my heart, for the fact that I am."

I clasped his hand, which was still every bit as callused and strong as my own and maybe more so in spite of the fact that this was the oldest age I'd ever seen him revealed to me, and I nodded to him in return. I still didn't understand what he meant and I didn't trust my own voice to thank him. But I did thank him inside.

Then he went back to his desk and picked up the Bible. It wasn't from Revelations that he read, though. It was from some place I think back in the Old Testament I'd never heard preached about before, and his voice broke a little and he wiped his eyes as he spoke the words:

The voice of my beloved!

Behold, he cometh leaping upon the mountains,

Skipping upon the hills.
My beloved is like a roe or a young hart;
Behold, he standeth behind our wall,
He looketh forth at the windows,
Showing himself through the lattice.
My beloved spake, and said unto me,
Rise up, my love, my fair one, and come away...

CHAPTER SEVEN

"Sounds like they're gettin' ready to bring him out," Big Jim muttered. "I'm a-takin' the quickest way home today."

Frank and John dismounted, their insides fluttering. They looked at each other, each harboring the thought of how they could ask Uncle Jim to stay with their horses so they could run and watch the execution. Both cleared their throats uncomfortably and blushed. But it was too late; Big Jim had already swung his horse around and started off.

He halted and turned around suddenly, though. "Frank!" he called, his first address of the morning to Hen's foster son.

"Yes sir?" Frank answered, finally finding his tongue.

"You tell ye daddy I'll be up on Greasy to see him afore long, all right? I'm thinkin' about buyin' some land down in Rowan County, and gettin' off the Big Sandy for good. Thought he might want to ride down with me to look at it. I could help him if he had some cattle he had to take to Flemingsburg or somethin'."

"Rowan County?" queried Frank, sounding a little more confident now but looking backward over his shoulder at the city. He turned his head to face Hen's big brother again. "But Uncle Jim, hain't they a lot of fightin' down that way right now too?"

"Yeah, they is, just some more of them no-accounts that Knott keeps a-pardonin' all over the hills, but it's fightin' I didn't start and I don't aim to finish. My partisan days is over. I just wanna go someplace I can live." He spurred his horse and started away again.

"Yes sir, I'll be shore to tell him," Frank called to his uncle's broad, retreating back. He looked at his companions.

"C'mon, boys, we gotta git, they'll have him strung up afore we know it!" he

cried. "These nags'll be all right here, let's just let 'em graze. It cain't be too different here than how it is on Greasy."

Lee Viers had remained mounted, and now, very pale-faced and still swallowing repeatedly, he swung down from his father's big horse, pulled his makeshift feed sack saddle off the animal's back, and draped it over his left shoulder.

"You go on, boys," he muttered, not looking at them. "I got about half a sack of middlin's here, and I'll take the brutes down the river bank and feed and water 'em. I'll stay here."

"Lee, you dauncy about the stomach or what? You all right?"

"Frank, I said I'd stay and take care of these brutes," Lee grated harshly between his teeth, still with his back turned. *"Somebody got to.* You'ns go on."

Frank shook his head in wonder and contempt, and in the same move he had seen Hen make ever since his childhood he slapped his own thigh. "Jesus Christ," he growled at his younger brother-in-law, "Here me and John has lugged you along with us all the way to Floyd County, and now you tell me you're a-chickenin' out? Sheeyit." That was the way the men on Greasy spoke the word when they were disgusted with something, and a cloud of mockery fairly arose from it like the stench from the real article.

Lee turned on Frank in sudden anger, the terror careening around inside his head and chest latching onto a legitimate manly outlet like a drowning man grasping a rope. "Dammit, Frank, you listen here," he rasped as he stamped his feet, "Mary alw's could outwork me but I'll be goddamned if that means you can put on like my big brother. You go on and watch your damn hangin' and I hope you don't piss your britches like a three year-old a-doin' it. You tend to ye own damn horse, I'm a-goin' home." With a yank to his mount's bridle that brought a whinny of protest from the beast, he turned his back on Frank and John and started leading the horse in the direction from whence they had come, too enraged and frightened to remember to gather his dignity and swing himself up on the mare's back.

The last thing that Frank remembered clearly before John managed to wrestle him backward was a rosy glow around Lee's retreating form. When he did come to his senses John was between him and Lee, exerting all his strength to hold him and gasping words of calm in his ear as if Frank were a fractious stallion he was trying to settle. White as a sheet, Lee remained utterly quiet and safely behind his mare's large bulk; for his part Frank emitted a jumble of unintelligible growls as John rasped in his ear, "Jesus God, Frank, you want to wind up in the same

cell tonight that Finley's just now gittin'
out of? Ca'm down! Ca'm it, good Lord,
your eyes are a-poppin' right out of your
head!"

After what seemed like an eternity,
Frank managed to slow his breathing and
bring his eyes back into focus. He turned
his head and stared weirdly a moment at
John, who was still straining to hold him
back and growling, "What the hell you
think's gonna happen one of these days
when I ain't around to hold you back?
You're gonna kill somebody yet, Frank, I
ain't never seen a temper on a man like
you've got. You think the people in this
town is gonna put up with you actin' like
this? You get ca'm and do it right

now...Frank? It's all right...it's all right, Frank, settle down."

Frank broke away from John, staggered a little further backward, and rubbed the middle of his back; often a spell of rage made him hurt there and in his pelvis, especially if he didn't get to vent his temper against anything or anybody else. "I'm all right now," he mumbled lowly to both John and Lee.

John took charge now and handled it well for his nineteen years. He turned to Lee. "Now, Lee, you listen here," he commanded as he caught his breath and began to savor his dignity as an arbitrator. "Nobody says you got to go to the hangin,' all right? You just stay right here and tend

to our horses if you want. It's gonna be a right rough mess just like Uncle Jim says and to tell you the truth I'm a little bit dauncy right now myself. You ain't the only one." On an impulse he winked at Lee and forced a brief smile to his face.

The empathy had its desired effect and Lee nodded at John gratefully, venturing out from behind the mare with wary eyes toward Frank. John continued as he turned his head, "Frank, ain't nobody sayin' you ain't a beardog, you hear me? Neither Lee nor me can take you on and we both know it and we don't want to. Right, Lee? Lee never meant no slur to you, him and me is both just wrought up and—and a bit scared. I admit it. Now you got your senses in hand enough for you and me to git on up in town before the hangin' is all over, and let Lee take the horses and stay close here?"

Frank nodded his head slightly and before he could control it his thick upper lip folded back on itself in an open, shamefaced grin. "Aw, shit, I'm sorry, Lee," he muttered as he held out his hand. "Too hot-headed, I reckon." His younger brother-in-law took the offered hand, returning the smile in genuine relief.

John slapped Frank on the shoulder. "Well, come on, then," he cried as he started off, "they're gonna have him strung up afore we can make it up there to see!"

Frank didn't have to be told twice. Holding his broad-brimmed black hat atop his head with his hand, he sprinted after John for the center of Prestonsburg as fast as his legs would take him.

CHAPTER EIGHT

...Ohhhh, she jumped in bed
And covered up her head
And swore I could not find her
But I knew damn well
She lied like hell
'Cause I jumped right in behind her
My calling is a minister
The virgins I do cherish
And I've got five boys
and seven little girls
Runnin' all around the parish...

Oh, good God have mercy. What a

way to wake up, with the two young

drunks that Jim Layne had to throw in the

cell next door, trying to sing "The Girl I Left

Behind Me" as loud and as dirty as they

can. One of the turnkeys rapped his billy

club across their cell bars and roared at

them to shut up. I flinched at the sound

and rubbed my eyes but the little sots just

giggled and laughed and blackguarded

back at him. Well, I suppose they can leave
town today or tomorrow or whenever Jim or
the sheriff decides to let them out, and they
can say that they gave Gus Finley a final
sendoff. I can't judge them really, either.
Who was it said that Gus will shoot, after
all?

I rubbed my aching neck and looked
out the cell window again. The sun was
high in the sky now, and I remembered
how crazy I'd gotten when the preachers
had come in with Harmon Harris and
brought my new clothes to me. I'd paced
and paced and paced back and forth and
back and forth through the cell like a caged
animal and tried to hold back from
screaming and crying. It was the worst

panic I'd took since the first night here after my sentence. But the preachers all tried to talk to me and calm me down and explain that the Lord works in mysterious ways and all things work together so just trust him, and after they'd laid hands on me and had prayer with me and I'd bawled and slung snot like a big baby for a while I managed to calm down enough to get my new suit and shoes on. Nice black broadcloth trousers, vest, coat, and shirt, but no collar nor tie. I looked good enough to bury. I'd have loved to make a joke about that to Mr. Harris or maybe Sol, but I wouldn't let myself. A sense of humor only goes so far, and Mr. Harris was almost as grieved over me as he would have been over one of his own sons.

I remember sitting down near as I could to the window, listening to the crowd gathering in the street and singing hymns around it and some of the preachers mixed in with the singers still trying to exhort to me. I had my Thomas Hymns on my lap looking up some of the songs they were singing to try to take my mind off the big lump of terror that was laying like a dead weight in the middle of my chest, and I guess it was then that I leaned forward and somehow dozed off while I was sitting there. For all I know it could have been that I fainted instead. I didn't have any idea how long I had catnapped or been out or whatever, or if I'd not fainted even how I'd managed to get to sleep. I was glad, though, that I got to dream about the

Professor one last time. Whoever or

whatever he is, he's truly been my friend.

My head and my heart pounded.

Everything felt so unreal that it was hard to

tell whether I was still dreaming or whether

I wasn't. As my mind raced along it

seemed more and more like just another

dream as the minutes went by. But then

Jim Layne and the turnkeys all came back

to my cell door with Mr. Harris and the

preachers in a big group, and when I saw

one of the turnkeys carrying a pair of hand

shackles and another with a big old thick

saddle girth strap with a buckle, I knew

finally it was time. I figured Jake Hollifield

would come with them too since he was in

charge of all this, but he wasn't there. He

must have stayed at the scaffold, maybe to let the crowd get a good look at him.

I left my Bible and hymnbook on my bench and asked Jim Layne if he'd please let Sol heir them from me, and he nodded very kindly and told me he would. I let them shackle my wrists behind me and lead me out the cell door, and then it didn't seem like it was but a few seconds that I was out of the jail and up in a wagon past the courthouse to the gallows with the soldiers marching ahead of us and the crowd yelling and singing and crying to beat the band all the while I was just riding along. I took a good long breath of the warm spring air and tried to look all around me. The spicewood and dogwood

blossoms up on the hillsides had started to
fade a bit but most of the other trees were
only starting to bud out. It was a time of
birth, and here I was going to die.

The last thing the Professor told me
before he shook hands with me in the
dream was to seek the truth, and to try to
make a difference. I still didn't see how I
could manage that, but if nothing else I
guessed I could tell people to heed my
example and not do no murder and avoid
my fate. It didn't sound like much. I didn't
know whether or not that was good enough
for God, but like the Professor said, what
other choice did I have at this point? No
sooner than I had walked the gauntlet
between the soldiers and climbed up the

thirteen steps and reached the trap door
than Jake, who didn't speak to me so much
as once, marched over with a swagger and
pulled the girth strap off the one turnkey's
shoulder and starting tying up my ankles
with it. I knew I had to do something to
keep my legs from shaking and myself from
panicking again, so I sang a hymn.

Everybody seemed to listen. As I was
singing I could see Sol out in the crowd and
even Vina and a lot of the folks that I'd
talked to when they let me sweep the
streets back in the fall and winter and
early spring. Aunt Sally and Vina were
both crying on Sol's shoulders and him and
a lot of the others were sobbing too, and
though it may be selfish of me to say so, I

was glad of it. Maybe I really had made a difference to somebody, for some reason I'd be missed, and maybe that was enough to meet my end with.

It was hard not to lose faith again, though. The shackles were so tight they started to make my hands hurt and turn numb. And whether or not the Professor actually believes in the devil, towards the end of the song and right before they let me speak I could have sworn I saw him pop his head out of the earth close to one of the wagons on the right side of the gallows.

CHAPTER NINE

"Thanks for that," muttered Frank breathlessly to John as he caught up with him.

"Aw, hell, somebody got to keep you offen the gallers yeself," John puffed back. "I ain't... givin' you no hard time over it... and don't you give Lee no more neither. You said you was... gonna get Mary a pipe, didn't ye?" he gasped, hoping for a change of subject.

"Have to wait till atter the hangin'," Frank huffed in return. "Got a couple coins and I reckon it's enough...it ain't, I'll trade my ol' pocketknife for one."

The dirt streets and badly warped board sidewalks were empty now except for tethered horses, mules, wagons, drunks passed out along the thoroughfare, and perhaps a quiet sneak thief or two looking for an unlocked store; everybody had crowded up beyond the main avenue to watch the festivities. When the boys reached the end of the main street the gallows suddenly loomed large from the farther edge of the pressing, jostling crowd, out in the open perhaps five hundred yards away from the dirty-looking little jail and not far from an ornate but somehow shabby building that had to be the courthouse. The branches of every tree in the area were jammed full of men and boys, to the point that several of the Divine in the midst of a very earthy world."

"Then all that leaves me is to try to seek truth, and to make a difference for somebody. And what kind of difference can I make for anybody now, Professor?"

He smiled again, just softly, and this time he didn't try to hide it.

"You should never stop looking for the chance, Augustus," he said. "You might be surprised. But what other course of action does either of us have at this point? What's done is done. What's done cannot be undone. But this doesn't mean necessarily that what is to be will be, in spite of the fact that most of the people here in our mountains have let that tired old proverb completely rot their minds away. If things were predetermined to that degree, we'd still have to act as if they weren't simply to get anything accomplished at all. But our time, yours—and—mine is short. Shall we read some more, perhaps something from the Book of Books this time, about the coming of the Lord Jesus?"

If there's any part of the Bible that sends me into a cold dread, it's the Book of Revelation, with all the brimstone and wormwood and suffering and cursing and torturing and dying and beasts eating you and the fire burning your skin off and everything going on, and after he asked that I thought sure it was what he was looked as if they must be brought down altogether by their human cargo. Frank and John could hear a vibrant, clear voice singing a minor-keyed hymn somewhere up near the crowd's center.

"Looks almost like a 'sociation, don't it, Frank?" John asked, blowing hard as they stopped up short at the edge of the crowd. They were so far back they couldn't tell which of the several men walking or standing on the scaffold was the guest of honor.

"Yeah, sounds like it too," Frank returned as he caught his breath. His real father had only the year before hosted an association meeting at his church, and Frank, who was then living with an

extremely pregnant Mary at Wash and
Cynthia Viers' cabin on Hurricane, had
attended the opening day of the function
and happened to see a couple of his real
mother's brothers there as representatives
of Martin and Pike County congregations.
Ashamed, he had trudged back to Wash
Viers' before they could catch sight of him;
according to the rules of hospitality he
would have been obliged to ask them to
dinner if he met them, and given his
status he didn't think he could very well
impose in that way on his in-laws. He
never thought of how his biological father
might have felt about receiving them as
guests in his church. But Cynthia Viers,
who had the reputation of being more
clever at her dinner table than anyone in

the community even though she cooked only out of a fireplace, had surprised him. When she heard what he had done, she ordered him to get right back down that creek and bring his two uncles up to eat at her table. He'd done so, and he and his wife's and his mother's people had had a pleasant time visiting both at the association grounds and at Wash Viers' packed little cabin. Frank had heard that very same mournful song now being sung as a solo, lined out to the association crowd by his real father the previous fall.

"Must be a preacher up there now with Finley," he whispered to John, "a-tryin' to sing to him and work with his soul. They wouldn't be so cruel as to hang

a man without bein' shore they was
sendin' him to heaven first."

Together, they listened to the
singer's rendition of the old song:

> *When sorrows encompass me round,*
> *And many distresses I see,*
> *Astonished, I cry, can a mortal be*
> *found,*
> *Surrounded with troubles like me?*

"Psst, Frank," John returned, "let's
take a sneak around the side of the crowd
and try and get a better look."

John walked rapidly but stealthily
on the route he had pointed to his
companion and Frank followed him
silently, captivated by the quavering but
clear unseen voice, so much like his real

father's but thinner and somehow

younger:

> *O, when will my sorrows subside?*
> *O, when shall my sufferings cease?*
> *O, when to the bosom of Christ be*
> *conveyed*
> *In the mansions of glory and bliss?*

Together, they rounded the crowd as

quickly as they dared, the song steadily

increasing in volume as they paced on.

Tall rifles with fixed bayonets were visible

above the crowd's heads at the upper side;

Frank knew they belonged to the state

militia standing guard, and he could see

that John understood that too, for he

stopped, indicating he knew they had to

be about as close as they were going to

get. They were still too far from the

scaffold to see what was going on, but the

plaintive voice rang louder:

> *My spirit to glory conveyed,*
> *My body laid low in the ground,*
> *I wish not a tear at my grave to be*
> *shed,*
> *Let all join in praising around.*

They passed the edge of the crowd

at the side of the scaffold, trying to inch in

closer, but were suddenly stopped short

by a thickly-mustached militiaman

holding his rifle at port arms.

"Nobody up here but officials," the

soldier growled at them *sotto voce.* "You

boys git back."

"Yes sir," John replied obligingly,

and took a surprised and disconcerted

Frank's arm and began to walk slowly backward.

"Frank," he hissed quietly, "when I say go, let's dive under that wagon over there fast. We can see out from under it."

"What wa—"

"Go!" John's whisper suddenly cut as the militiaman turned around. Without thinking or seeing but following John's lead, Frank quickly dropped to hands and knees and scooted under the black enclosed wagon with his companion, the two of them peering out cautiously between the legs of one or two well-dressed men standing on the other side of it. Another boy who had already sought

the same vantage point greeted them with a grin and scooted over.

"Ruint my good coat and vest and britches," Frank muttered bitterly, feeling dampness on his right waist and thigh as he tried to twist sideways to get his feet under the conveyance. John made similar motions silently. Frank looked around and realized where they had crawled.

"John," he hissed, "this is the undertaker's wagon, I think, I seen one in Paintsville! I bet you them's undertakers right in front of us—"

"*Shh!* They'll hear you. I know. It was all we could do. Look up there."

Frank listened and looked toward the gallows:

> *If souls disembodied can know,*
> *Or visit their brethren beneath,*
> *My spirit shall join you while singing*
> *you go,*
> *And leave all my cares in the grave.*

They had a middling view now if they craned their necks a bit, with most of the gallows clearly visible. But it was an excellent vantage point for the underside of the scaffold, and they could even see the big strap hinges of the trapdoor in the center of the structure as well as the fixtures supporting the iron bar that held it closed. With the exception of that trapdoor, the lever above and behind it on the top surface that was fastened to the end of the bar protruding beneath, and the high crossbeam with its dangling noose, the scaffold did bear an eerie resemblance to the crude homemade stages cobbled together for outside services at Baptist association meetings, even to the number of men standing and milling about on it. There was a young and well-dressed but pale and hollow-eyed fellow just about where the moderator ought to be, a couple of paces or so behind the center front of the structure and obviously squarely on the trapdoor, leading the mournful minor-keyed song. But it was certainly no preacher; his hands appeared to be bound tightly behind his back, and Frank could see a thick leather belt doubled and buckled around his ankles.

Gus Finley the murderer, himself, Frank realized with a chill as he thought of the verse the boy had just sung. If Gus's soul, disembodied, did come back to the earth, would it be the benign presence that the mournful Baptist tearjerker hymn seemed to imply, or a malevolent ghost bent on revenging its torments on those who had come to gawk at its temporal suffering? The sweet tenor rose again to bring the minor-keyed melody to a close:

> *Immersed in the ocean of love,*
> *My soul like an angel shall sing,*
> *Till Christ shall descend with a shout*
> *from above,*
> *And make all Creation to ring.*

The boy cleared his throat, spat on the stage, licked his dry lips, and began to speak. The wind played a bit with his hair, though with bound hands he had no means to straighten it. Despite Frank's closeness he couldn't catch all of Gus's farewell address; it appeared to be devoid of emotion, neither repentant nor defiant but a simple statement of the boy's belief that he was being made an example of, and that he was the first and would be the last man ever hanged in Floyd County. Then Gus abruptly turned his face sideways and addressed one of the somber men standing there.

"Jake," he said quietly, "my hands hurt me. Let's get this over with." That at least, Frank could hear plainly.

A great buzz arose from the crowd. Lying in this position Frank couldn't see the reactions of very many, but those he did view appeared to be as white-faced and hollow-eyed as was the boy himself. Someone stumblingly read from a document up on the stand and did an extremely poor job of pronouncing most of the bigger words. An older man in a neat suit, his countenance ravaged by grief he could hardly conceal, put a hand on Gus's shoulder and whispered something in his ear, to which the boy did not reply. Frank now recognized Harmon Harris, the defense attorney; Hen had once pointed Harris out to him, when they'd been on a cattle-buying trip down on Big Sandy.

Then Harris and all the other men but Gus and the lone deputy whom he had addressed stepped as far away from the trapdoor as they could, and the deputy grabbed the noose, brought it near, and tightened it around Gus's neck. Gus flinched involuntarily, but remained composed and tight-lipped. A long low feminine wail arose from somewhere back in the crowd. Frank, whose own neck already had a crick in it from the odd angle he was forced to maintain, realized with another shudder that for all anyone knew, the voice very well could have been that of Gus's mother, his sister, or his sweetheart.

The executioner then proceeded to affix some sort of black covering over Gus's head. It was too small to be called a hood really, and it concealed only his face and the upper part of his head almost like an oversized cap, which in fact it may have been. Frank's thoughts raced back to what Uncle Jim had said. If this hanging was done right, Gus's neck would break and he would die quickly and mercifully; if it wasn't he'd smother to death slowly, the face turning as black as the cap that covered it, the eyes and tongue gorged with purple vein-blood to the point of bursting. Everybody knew that without being told. Frank gnawed at his deformed upper lip and scraggly mustache with his lower teeth again. For a second he almost got the lunatic notion that his mustache was somehow his own personal version of a black cap.

CHAPTER TEN

Time is such a funny thing... Odd, I mean, not humorous... I know it's not been fifteen or twenty seconds since Jake hooded my face and yet I've been able to remember and recite every single detail of my last morning in that short space: all the happenings, all the talk, and even the dreams and nightmares. How does time work? How can a few seconds seem so long sometimes and then an hour be so short at others? I had a whole eternity in front of my eyes... in my memories... just from this morning... I'm about to go to the place where time shall be no more, and I've never figured it out and now I never will...

I wish I'd picked out a better hymn. I always did hate that sympathy kind and I don't know why that one stuck in my mind the way it did. I wish my last words had sounded better and more like poetry the way the Professor always could make his... I didn't even say I was sorry that Jimmy was dead though I surely am but it doesn't seem right now to holler out anything else and add more words or take any back... I made the prophecy that I'd be the last man that would ever be hanged in Floyd Count. Pray God... I'm not going to my death with a lie on my lips. I reckon I sounded better than whoever it was that read my sentence out to the crowd. If I could just get this notion out of my head that this is all a dream and it's not really happening... I'm just standing here

waiting:

WAITING OH JESUS GOD

Jimmy I am so sorry. I know I said
that Gus will shoot but I wouldn't have had
this happen to you for the world. Maybe I
can tell you that face to face in a minute...
Maybe I can see Bill James and little Susan
too and we can all smile happy and tell one
another how this just seemed to us like a
bad nightmare. Maybe... THERES TOO
MANY GODDAMNED MAYBES! LORD GOD
HAVE MERCY, FORGIVE ME FOR THEM
PROFANE WORDS! I WANT TO RUN SO
BAD... JESUS GIT ME OUTA THIS!

My hands are killing me. They hurt
so bad I'm trying to breathe through this
cap in great big lungfuls and my ears roar

and my temples are pounding and my heart's so far up in my throat I can feel my pulses scratch rope on both sides every time my heart gives a beat! Jesus, Jesus, I'm so scared I'll piss on myself or worse like they say dying men do but I'm in such a shape there's no way I can piss right now, I am so glad nobody can see my face! God help me! I am such a confused and mixed up mess of muscle and bone and blood and spunk and nerves...

What was it that Jesus said? Father, into thy hand I commend my spirit... Or did he just say it is finished? I think one book says one thing and another says another. Which one's right? If somehow I could just know that I had the truth of things and that I'd made a difference... Oh Jesus! Jesus...

Jesus... JESUS... JESUS... JESUS...

JESUS...

FATHER INTO MY HAND I

COMMEND.... THY SWEET LORD JESUS...

HAVE MERCY... LIE DOWN ON MY

COUCH...TO PLEASANT IS IT FINISHED...

THE VOICE OF MY BELOVED

BEHOLD HE COMETH A-SKIPPIN' ON THE

HILLS... ARISE MY...

NOOOOOOO! NO! NO! NOOO... NOT

THIS TIME! NO, NOT NOW GODDAMN YOU!

YOU WON'T GET AWAY WITH IT SO HELP

ME GOD IF IT'S THE LAST THING I EVER

DO I'LL...

IF I COULD JUST GIT TURNED BACK

AROUND TO... IF SOULS DISEMBODIED

CAN KNOW AND VISIT THEIR

BRETHREN... OH BLESS HIS LITTLE SOUL

HE'S ALL RIGHT NOW... OHHHHH THANK

YOU LORD! JESUS COME QUICKLY HAVE

MER—

    PROFESSOR!—

CHAPTER ELEVEN

Frank wished there was a bush somewhere close. He angrily clenched his sphincter muscle tight as he realized what his nerves were doing to him. He reminded himself he was a grown man and a father now, and he must act the part and hold it in. He'd dive somewhere back down over the riverbank and find a spot where he could relieve himself in a few minutes. His own neck throbbed again with a muscle spasm.

Up on the scaffold, the deputy in charge of the killing, Frank had observed, was visibly trembling for all his hoped-for bravado as he took hold of the trapdoor lever. He had jerked it back viciously as if a Herculean effort were necessary to move it, and a great shout had arisen from the crowd again as Gus dropped. In spite of himself, Frank had blinked his eyes at the sound of the bar's rasp and the trap's release, but he opened them to see the body of the condemned man reach the end of the rope. The shouting grew louder for an instant and subsided as quickly as if it had been a candle blown out by a higher power; now calls of distress and anger were heard interspersed with curses, and the entire crowd seemed to move involuntarily backward. Many were turning away, Frank could see as he twisted his aching neck around, and he could smell the acrid stink of vomit seemingly rising up in the air from all directions. He tightened his abdomen again and focused his eyes on the underside of the scaffold once more. And then he knew the cause of the crowd's reaction...

The rope was too long. Just as Big Jim had warned Frank, John and Lee some few moments before, telling them the special deputy in charge of the hanging did not know a thing about what he was doing, it was evident that he was incompetent. The tips of Gus Finley's shoes were touching the ground and his body with its black-capped face and bound limbs twisted and contorted grotesquely and horribly, twirling around and then back again as he sought without

hope to gain one last hold on the earth
with his tied feet. Women screamed and
some fainted and male voices arose,
almost comical in their panic:

*"Gus! Gus! Honey, bring ye knees up
to ye chest and jerk 'em back down hard!
Git this over with, honey! Oh, Lord have
mercy God!"*

*"Somebody do somethin'! Pull on his
legs! Pull on his legs!"*

*"Oh, God, are you gonna have to
take him back up there and try this again?"*

*"Ye're a big man now, Jake
Hollifield! Now ever' body's gonna be
scared of such a big tough hangman, that
what you wanted?"*

Jake leapt from the scaffold to the ground, spat, and swallowed, his face white as chalk.

"Fetch ye shovels all over here! *Now!*" he roared in the direction of the wagon under which Frank and John lay. The team of horses at the upper end, spooked, stamped their feet and nickered, and the frame of the hearse shook over them. The pair of legs partially blocking their view seemed to tangle with one another as the two undertakers scrambled sideways to reach the horses and calm them. All the men remaining on top of the scaffold appeared to be trying to work with Harmon Harris, who looked like he had fainted dead away.

"We left the shovels all up at the graveyard!" shrieked the hysterical voice of one of the undertakers trying to hold the horses' reins.

The deputy swore horrible oaths, and demanded that somebody better open a store quick and get him a shovel. The smell underneath the wagon sharpened; John Addington was being actively and vigorously sick.

When he was done retching, he cleared his throat and moaned, "Oh, God, Frank, I cain't stand it! I'm goin' back with Lee, come on! He was right!"

"Lookut the front of his britches!" cackled the boy on his other side, turning to look at the cousins. "Hey, what's with you? Wait! Why, you got to hang around and smell him let go his death shit—"

"WILL YOU SHUT UP!" John cut him off hoarsely in a weird combination of a bellow and a gag, making a jittery, almost panicky motion to strike him. But the space under the wagon was cramped and John's arm, though strong and muscular, was just too shaky now to be of much effect. The boy dodged the blow easily as John raked knuckles on the underside of the wagon, cursed in return and wriggled further away, muttering about having the law on them but deciding, finally, to ignore them.

His abraded right hand dripping

blood, John rolled out from underneath

the wagon and half ran, half staggered,

back in the direction they had come, not

even waiting to see if Frank followed. By

now so many of the onlookers were fleeing

that the militiamen hardly even noticed

John. Frank did not accompany his

cousin. His eyes were fixed on Gus

Finley's *danse macabre*, and he realized he

would stay until the last steps were taken

and the bows made. Somebody managed

to procure a shovel for the deputy, and

Jake, stifling a retch at the odor that

Frank and John's companion under the

wagon had categorized so bluntly,

frantically scraped out a shallow hole

under Gus's feet. He stepped back,

swiping with a grimy hand at reddened
eyes as wide as silver dollars, and panted
in sobbing gasps after he had cleared two
inches or so of space between the tips of
the boy's toes and the ground. Gus
danced slower and ever slower over the
next several minutes, still twirling
clockwise and then counterclockwise, his
movements gradually degenerating into
involuntary twitches until he gave one last
great convulsive jerk and was still, the
rope swinging the corpse gently back and
forth. For whatever good it had
accomplished, the black cap still held
firmly over Gus's face.

Jake staggered back from the body
ready to be held up and steadied by the

pallid, frightened turnkeys. Another well-dressed man crept hesitantly under the scaffold, opened a black case he carried, withdrew what appeared to Frank to be a small weird-looking rubber and metal contraption, and seemed to try to stick parts of the thing in his ears and then to put the opposite end of it on Gus' chest. Frank jerked himself out of his fetal position and his near-catatonic state with a start. When they cut the boy down they'd have to move this wagon over nearer the gallows, and for all he knew it could start rolling at any minute. His and John's nameless companion had already crawled off somewhere else, apparently having had a jolly time out of the whole event. With an effort Frank angled back,

the pains from the stiffened muscles of his
legs and neck skyrocketing up and down
his spine, and he staggered to his feet to
face a top-hatted undertaker who was as
white and vacant-eyed as he was himself.
For just an instant he thought the man
would try to detain him, but the
undertaker simply looked right through
him and beyond. Perhaps he was thinking
of his next chore, removing that black cap
on Gus Finley's face, but Frank didn't wait
around to find out. He lurched as quickly
as he could back down the avenue he and
John Addington had run up an eternity
ago. Frank kept hoping that Lee had fed
and watered the horses and that he and
John would look for a secluded place
somewhere on the riverbank so he could

wash himself and his clothes at least partially. Frank ran thinking that and wondering how to keep John's mouth shut about his having to do it...

He shuddered again as he thought about washing himself in the river where Gus Finley and the night turnkey from the jail had gone swimming, perhaps even in the very hole of water where, only a few nights before, Gus and his youthful guard had ducked one another and maybe had talked about girls under a full moon...

CHAPTER TWELVE

The light of gray dawn shone dully though the open barn door, and Frank squinted a bit as he groped at the peg on the wall for the right size bridle for his horse.

'Pears looked like my harebrained boys have left the tack out of place again, Frank thought.

For the life of him he couldn't figure out why eleven- and nine- and seven-year old boys couldn't keep saddle tack and plow rigging in proper order; he couldn't recall being guilty of such a transgression himself at their ages, and he figured that Hen would have lambasted him if he had.

There were, however, a few things about the past that Frank could remember all too clearly for comfort. Almost eleven years had come and gone since Gus Finley's hanging, and Frank, John Addington, and Lee Viers had all apparently had their fill of such spectacles. Not one of them had shown any interest in making the journey back to Prestonsburg to see Gus's noose after it had been nailed up on display behind the judge's bench in the circuit courtroom of the Floyd County court house. Neither could any of them be persuaded to attend Jim Pud Marcum's hanging at Louisa to the north of Greasy Creek in 1887 or that of Ellison Mounts in Pikeville in 1890, even though the memory of Ellis Craft and the Ashland Tragedy had faded on Greasy Creek over time and in the eyes of their more curious neighbors the three were now old hands at this execution-visiting business and could have provided on-the-scene commentary for both events. And for reasons that none of them had ever proven willing to discuss, Frank, John, and Lee all had had an unusual amount of trouble sleeping at night as the dates of these two latter hangings had approached and become items of community gossip. They wouldn't have had to worry about at least one particular of eastern Kentucky criminal justice, though: after the Finley hanging, state courts handing down capital sentences now usually specified the construction of gallows with their undersides completely boxed in and covered, with only a door for access underneath. That is, at least for white criminals.

But Frank was on a different errand this morning. It was the fourteenth day of March 1896, and he was now the proprietor of his own farm up Yost Branch some distance from Hen and Jane. Since the birth of the oldest, Mary never had been one to complain much about her labor pains, and so when she had quietly informed him a few minutes earlier that he'd better ride down to the mouth of the branch and tell Maw Jane and Grandpa Fat to come up and stay with her while he went on over to Hurricane and got her mother, he had no doubt it was time.

Having already borne four strong boys and a girl, most of them with only Cynthia Viers on hand as a midwife, Mary knew what she was talking about. Frank rubbed the stubble on his unshaven cheeks and chewed a moment on his misshapen upper lip, now completely hidden behind a long, thick, bristly mustache, before he finally clutched the bridle he wanted.

Eleven year-old George, whom he had roused to come and help him, stood by his father and the horse. George leaned first on one foot and then the other, yawning and digging a small fist into one sleepy eye. As so often occurred with him after a hard day's work on the farm with his parents, the boy had experienced a couple of extremely vivid bad dreams the night before, one almost as soon as he'd dozed off on his tick and another a deep night-terror during the wee hours that woke his parents and brothers Henderson, James, and John and even his sister Nancy Jane. His drawn face showed the effects of both the farm labor and the nightmares.

"Here, George," Frank muttered, "come up forenst and steady the horse's head. You had this bridle on the wrong peg. You have a care how you hang it up from now on, you hear me?"

"Y-y-y-yes sir, I'm s-sorry," the boy stammered, not out of any particular fear, though he knew his father was already irked at him this early, but simply because he had a persistent and pronounced stutter that seemingly nothing could break. His mother blamed the speech impediment on Grandpa Fat's habit of tickling George when he was a tiny boy, but whatever caused it, one had to strain to understand any long sentence that the child tried to say. For all that, he was bright and so far had done very well in his annual five-month terms of school, the time between corn laying-by in July and the snows of December. Already he was talking about becoming a schoolteacher when he grew up—that is, when he could manage to force such a long word out of his mouth in one try.

He'll never make it with that stutter, Frank thought disgustedly as he chewed on his lip again. *Schoolteachers have to talk all day, and talking is pert nigh the toughest thing for George to do. Boy can't grow hair or put on clothes to cover up a thing like that. And him not having enough common sense to know where to put that damn bridle, and them dreams and nightmares two or three nights out of the week—well, something has to be done about him soon, no question.*

The horse, a fine, well-fed seven year-old mare that could pull a plow all day and carry a saddle afterward with the best of the breed, now proved high-spirited and intractable. As Frank tried to fasten the cavalry bridle, she shook and tossed her head with an irritated nicker and a snap of her teeth. Frank's mood had already clouded dangerously during his search for the bridle, and between that and the memory of George's nightmares and his apprehension about the birth of a sixth child his temper exploded. His face contorted in a rage he could not control as he raised the bridle up, aiming to strike the animal across its broad back, but he stopped the motion in midair. He couldn't afford to let the iron bit or even a ring or buckle on the bridle gash the horse. If he did so, he couldn't ride her till her back healed, and he had to get to Hurricane fast. Clenching bridle leather tightly in his fist, he looked about wildly for a vent for the fury that had overtaken him. Once, years before, he had nearly broken his knuckles by hitting a barn wall in response to an almost identical situation.

This morning he had a more convenient target—one much more familiar, as well.

If he hadn't been so sleepy, little George, who was trying his best to steady the horse's head from the other side, might have seen it coming. As it was, he jerked back in shock and pain as one of the eye hooks of the bridle bit struck him on the ball joint of his left shoulder as his father swung with all his might across the beast's neck. Had the mare not been in the way, his shoulder might have been broken rather than badly bruised. He back stepped, his hands flying instinctively to cover his face and neck, wailing, "Wha— Wha— Wha—"

"You little tongue tied pup, I told you to hold that brute steady!" Frank roared. The horse, now completely spooked, dropped her head with a terrified whinny and stumbled backward in a wild tangle of hooves, knocking back Frank's arm and hand as she did. As soon as she was free of both Frank and the boy, she turned tail and bolted through the open barn door, breaking into a gallop.

"Well, goddamn it to hell! Look at this now, that damn bridle... and now I've got to run and catch that horse and your mommy's gone to bed with a *baby!*" Frank's voice rose to a harsh crescendo. Swinging the lethal weapon that the bridle had become in his hand, he eyed his oldest son malevolently. George fled to the barn wall and cowered sideways, his hurt shoulder pressed against hewn log, hiding his head, face, and neck as best he could behind his hands, knowing well, much, much too well, what was coming.

The boy had learned never to question the reasons, or the lack thereof, for his father's unpredictable violence. The same man who continually urged him to do well at school, who had once packed a big coffee sack full of Irish potatoes horseback all the way down to the mouth of Lick Creek on Big Sandy to find a merchant willing to trade a *McGuffey's First Reader* for the vegetables. The same man who had tenderly carried him home on his shoulders when he had accidentally gashed his foot with a hatchet while they were woodcutting five years ago, that man was also the uncaring monster who had tricked George and his next-oldest brother, Henderson, into breaking open a nest of yellow jackets and had laughed heartily about the boys' stings, pain, and tears. That same man could strike his sons and his daughters alike with the insane fury of a wild beast whenever something went slightly wrong or the urge happened to take hold of him. All George knew was that Grandpa Fat, Grandma Jane, Grandpa Wash, Grandma Cynthia, his uncles Lee, Jeff, Jack, and John, and his aunt Nancy were kind to him; that his mother Mary, continually busy both with child-bearing and house and farm work, simply believed that young ones had to be tough and endure their share of hardships to earn their *raisin'*, as she so often put it.

George had a hard time telling when it was safe to get in his father's way or keep his distance. The man's temper was the boy's reality, and as a child will, he accepted it as he found it.

If only Grandpa Fat were in the barn now, though, he'd wave his arms and bellow, *"Come to Grampaw, consarn it, George, come to Grampaw, consarn it!"* and if George could reach him he would be safe for the moment. But Grandpa Fat wasn't here, and he'd just have to take his lumps until Frank's anger was spent.

Even so, though his terror made it hard to think, this morning George was intelligent enough to realize that he was in more danger than usual. If any of the metal rings, or especially the bit, on that bridle happened to strike him just at the right angle on the temple or behind the ear, the impact could kill him. He knew that. From some quarter of his racing mind a song, one that he had heard down at the meetinghouse below the forks of the creek from the old preacher that looked so uncannily like his father, entered his thoughts. He could hear the minor-keyed tune clearly, but the words were garbled.

Something about souls disembodied can know and visit their brethren on earth, he thought.

Those words, at least, were almost physically audible. Perhaps his paralyzing fear, so intense that he couldn't even feel his bruised shoulder anymore, was making his imagination play tricks on him; or worse, it was a sign that his time had finally come. He closed his eyes, swallowed, and braced himself for what would follow, an agony he didn't even want to imagine.

But it happened on this late winter morning in 1896 that, as the words of the mournful Baptist hymn wafted through George's mind, he heard the bridle drop from his father's hand with a clink of metal and a swish of leather onto the soft straw next to him. When he finally ventured to uncover his eyes and look at his surroundings, he allowed his terror-numbed body to relax, but he could still hardly control the spasms of his abdominal muscles.

Silhouetted by the gray dawn through the open barn door, his father was staring wide-eyed and white-faced at a corner of the barn faintly illumined by the eerie dawn light. He kept opening and closing his mouth and swallowing rapidly as his fists clenched and unclenched.

It's happened again, George knew. *That thing Poppie talks about so often around the fireplace on long winter evenings... That thing he says he sees in the dark of the barn and in the woods every once in a while. It's here.*

This time, George would survive.

Frank looked weirdly at his son and then once again down at the bridle. In a motion that made little George flinch anew, the man suddenly kicked the implement with all his strength into the opposite corner of the barn, provoking an aggrieved lowing from the cow whose flank it had missed by a hairsbreadth.

When Frank spoke once more it was almost a whisper, with deep breaths every few words: "I alw's wondered why that kept happenin'," Frank croaked. "And it ain't till this day I could ever tell. Jesus Christ, I coulda killed you just now, George, and I'm durn fool enough to have done it but fer that..."

He gesticulated haphazardly and shakily at nothing George could see and gulped hard, almost audibly, then looked once more at the blanched face of his eldest son. His eyes kept going back to the darkened barn corner, and he would shudder as if he'd taken a mouthful of freshly pickled, uncooked and unwashed sauerkraut and been forced to swallow it down whole.

George, a diminutive figure at the barn wall, was still almost too intimidated to move, let alone answer. He stared warily back at his father like some small wild animal, trying to breathe slowly and shallowly for fear even of making that much motion. Frank suddenly reached out an enormous roughened hand and rubbed it over his son's head; almost completely unused to gestures of affection from his father, the boy flinched once more, then nearly relaxed for an instant when he sensed that Frank was trembling now as well. Even so, George still didn't trust himself enough to speak.

"You keep that school up, you hear, George?" Frank finally said lowly, his thick, misshapen upper lip working nervously as he looked down. "I want you to be a better man than I ever have been. You want to be a teacher, you be one, but be a good one. You just start talkin' slower and try not to stutter and you'll make it. I sure as the world don't understand you sometimes, but I'm...I'm proud of you, son. I know I never told you that before, but I am. Way you love books, you're just different from me, I reckon. But if time goes on another year, atter the teacher closes the schoolhouse for Christmas and if I can find somebody a-runnin' a extry subscription school somewhere around here close enough, I promise you I'll pay your fee to go to it—even if I have to give Irish taters fer it just like that first readin' book that time. Maybe I can get Squire Hicks to board you. He sends his boys and girls both to schools like that, and some of them older Hicks boys is teachers already. Could be one of 'em'll do a school like that theirself this year..."

George could hardly believe his ears. He knew the local magistrate's sons well, though they lived far down on lower Greasy, and he had occasionally even ventured to pester one or the other of them to read or recite poems to him. The Hicks place, that fabled house of books and poetry and teachers, came close to his

own personal conception of heaven—
although the boys did have that one little
dark-haired sister about George's own age,
who could be so annoying...

"And when you grow up, when
people see you, I want 'em to be able to
say: 'Well, here comes the Professor,'"
Frank continued as he rubbed his hand
over his son's pate again, then the
shoulder he had injured, and almost drew
his thickened lip up over his teeth in a
crooked half-smile. "Not just an old dirt
farmer and cattle trader like me and your
grandpa is. 'Professor Harman,' what you
think about bein' called a name like that?"

To this suggestion George finally
responded, if ever so slightly: "Yes...sir,"
whispering, as he pulled himself erect next

to his father, hesitating briefly, but then speaking slowly and carefully to suppress his stammer, saying, "I'd...like that."

Suddenly Frank remembered what he had to do, and the pastoral moment was no more.

Still, he spoke more kindly than usual to his son. "Listen here, George," he said quietly, "I've gotta catch that horse and go get Maw Cinthy pretty quick. I can still ride bareback and hold to a rope halter, I reckon! And if I can't catch her, why, I'll just borry one of Grandpa Fat's and go on to Harrican, and him and Maw Jane'll be up through here in a few minutes. You go ahead and get some chop and feed the chickens and take the eggs in the house and just git things started till they show up, you hear? Maw Jane'll git up some breakfast, and the cows'll manage all right for now, I reckon. Either Grandpa Fat or me can milk 'em later on..."

George nodded his head slightly in assent, and then his father was out of the barn at a lope, pausing for one last nervous glance backward toward that one eerily-lit corner.

When he knew he was alone, George allowed himself the luxury of four or five great racking sobs before he forced the remainder of his fear and bewilderment deep down inside his chest. He staggered back to the barn wall for a moment, shakily unbuttoned his trousers, and released his bladder in a pile of straw. He wondered for a moment at the prospect of how long his father's kindness to him might last—the man's rare repentances, as well as his rages, were often unpredictable as to length—but he had no doubt whatsoever that he'd just come within a hairsbreadth of...of...something he'd never, ever, want to talk about. At least for many, many years...

For the briefest moment, though, George relaxed as he thought about the title of "Professor" and daydreamed about the subscription school this coming winter and the rest of his future. For a fleeting second, there, it very nearly seemed that he had somehow traveled forward in time to realize all of his ambitions and the joys and disappointments and griefs that were to accompany them, even if only in his mind and heart. He shook his head quickly and became eleven again, though, as he reminded himself that those dreams of his, both daytime and night varieties, were usually what got him into the most trouble. He buttoned his trousers and composed himself to scamper along to the chores Frank had assigned him, wincing a bit as he finally indulged himself in a rub to his hurt shoulder.

But before he left the barn, he paused briefly in heartfelt gratitude, returned his eyes to that one dark, eerie corner, and whispered his thanks to an unseen savior for the grace of a timely rescue: Frank Harman's recurring early-morning hallucination of Gus Finley's final, grotesque dance under the gallows.

For a moment George almost thought he could share his father's vision of a too-long rope twisting and jerking there within that darkened angle, and a contorting figure straining under a black cap drawn tightly across its face.

If souls disembodied can know,

And visit their brethren beneath...

Made in the USA
Charleston, SC
30 December 2015